Trained toge ~~...~~ **hese
six women** ~~...~~ **n in
need. Now o** ~~...~~ **ered,
and it is up to them to find the killer—
before they become the next victims....**

Alex Forsythe:
This forensic scientist can uncover clues others fail to see.
PROOF by Justine Davis—July 2004

Darcy Allen Steele:
A master of disguise, Darcy can sneak into
any crime scene.
ALIAS by Amy J. Fetzer—August 2004

Tory Patton:
Used to uncovering scandals, this investigative reporter
will get to the bottom of any story—especially murder.
EXPOSED by Katherine Garbera—September 2004

Samantha St. John:
Though she's the youngest, this lightning-fast secret agent
can take down men twice her size.
DOUBLE-CROSS by Meredith Fletcher—October 2004

Josie Lockworth:
A little danger won't stop this daredevil air force pilot
from uncovering the truth.
PURSUED by Catherine Mann—November 2004

Kayla Ryan:
The police lieutenant won't rest until the real killer is
brought to justice, even if it makes her the next target!
JUSTICE by Debra Webb—December 2004

ATHENA FORCE:
They were the best, the brightest, the strongest—
women who shared a bond like no other....

Dear Reader,

Welcome to Silhouette Bombshell, the hottest new line to hit the bookshelves this summer. Who is the Silhouette Bombshell woman? She's the bombshell of the new millennium; she's savvy, sexy and strong. She's just as comfortable in a cocktail dress as she is brandishing blue steel! Now she's being featured in the four thrilling reads we'll be bringing you each month.

What can you expect in a Silhouette Bombshell novel? A high-stakes situation in which the heroine saves the day. She's the kind of woman who always gets her man—and we're not just talking about the bad guy. Take a look at this month's lineup....

From *USA TODAY* bestselling author Lindsay McKenna, we have *Daughter of Destiny,* an action-packed adventure featuring a Native American military pilot on a quest to find the lost ark of her people. Her partner on this dangerous trek? The one man she never thought she'd see again, much less risk her life with!

This month also kicks off ATHENA FORCE, a brand-new twelve-book continuity series featuring friends bonded during their elite training and reunited when one of them is murdered. In *Proof,* by award-winning author Justine Davis, you'll meet a forensic investigator on a mission, and the sexy stranger who may have deadly intentions toward her.

Veteran author Carla Cassidy brings us a babe with an attitude—and a sense of humor. Everyone wants to *Get Blondie* in this story of a smart-mouthed cop and the man she just can't say no to when it comes to dealing out justice.

Finally, be the first to read hot new novelist Judith Leon's *Code Name: Dove,* featuring Nova Blair, the CIA's secret weapon. Nova's mission this time? Seduction.

We hope you enjoy this killer lineup!

Sincerely,

Natashya Wilson
Associate Senior Editor, Silhouette Bombshell

Please address questions and book requests to:
Silhouette Reader Service
U.S.: 3010 Walden Ave., P.O. Box 1325, Buffalo, NY 14269
Canadian: P.O. Box 609, Fort Erie, Ont. L2A 5X3

PROOF

JUSTINE DAVIS

BOMBSHELL™

Published by Silhouette Books

America's Publisher of Contemporary Romance

Special thanks and acknowledgment are given to Justine Davis for her contribution to the ATHENA FORCE series.

 SILHOUETTE BOOKS

ISBN 0-373-51316-X

PROOF

Visit Silhouette Books at www.eHarlequin.com

Printed in U.S.A.

JUSTINE DAVIS

lives in Kingston, Washington. Her interests outside of writing are sailing, doing needlework, horseback riding and driving her restored 1967 Corvette roadster—top down, of course. Justine says that years ago, when she worked in law enforcement, a young man she worked with encouraged her to try for a promotion to a position that was, at that time, occupied only by men. "I succeeded, became wrapped up in my new job and that man moved away, never, I thought, to be heard from again. Ten years later he appeared out of the woods of Washington State, saying he'd never forgotten me and would I please marry him. With that history, how could I write anything but romance?" And with a kick-ass career on the force, how could Justine not write a Silhouette Bombshell novel? Justine has put her police background to use to launch Silhouette Bombshell's twelve-book continuity, ATHENA FORCE, with *Proof*.

Chapter 1

I need your help.

Four small words, yet they had the power to turn an FBI agent into a burglar.

It had been a while, but Alexandra Forsythe quickly saw that the locks at the hospital, in this basement area anyway, were not going to be a particular challenge. The security of the small-town medical center wasn't designed to protect against people like her.

She was thankful the practice of observation had become so ingrained in her. As a forensic scientist with the FBI, she focused on tiny details every day, so even though she'd been here earlier under horrible circumstances, she was still able to recall most of what she needed now. The layout of the building, the basement and the morgue itself.

That she was risking her career with the FBI was something she was quite aware of. Yet, when placed on the opposite end of the scale from the woman who lay on the other side of this door, it didn't even move the dial.

Lorraine Miller Carrington had counted on that commitment when she'd put out the call invoking an old promise among friends. Alex had made the Cassandra promise with all the zeal of a passionate young woman, but her dedication to what it meant had never wavered as time passed. She would do what had to be done, whatever the cost. They all would, every one of the remaining six Cassandras. They would keep their word.

It was what graduates of the Athena Academy for the Advancement of Women did.

"Oh, God, Rainy," she murmured, feeling her eyes brim with the tears she had been fighting so hard all day.

Alex had come back to southern Arizona expecting trouble. She could only guess at the severity of the situation that would make the cool, unflappable Rainy put in that call for help. She knew it hadn't been done lightly.

But she had never expected to end up here, in the small town of Casa Grande, just north of the smaller town of Eloy, where Rainy's car had crashed. Rainy had made it only a third of the way from her home in Tucson to Athena Academy, just west of Phoenix. It was there where four of her former mentees, the Cassandras, had waited with Athena Academy principal Christine Evans to hear what dire event had instigated Rainy's desperate call.

Now Alex wondered if there could be anything worse than watching an autopsy on someone you loved.

She reined in her emotions and glanced up and down the hallway to be certain she was alone. Foot traffic down here was rare at 3:00 a.m. She'd waited in a shadowy side corridor until she'd seen a man with a cleaning cart load up with fresh supplies and get on an elevator. He was the third uniformed worker to have followed this route, and she was guessing from the fact that she'd seen three of the big carts in the storage room that he was the last of the night cleaning crew. Still, she waited a little longer, just to be sure.

Finally she slipped on the blue uniform smock she'd liberated from a linen closet on the third floor ward, figuring it might buy her a few seconds if she was discovered. Her intractable red-gold spiral curls were already pulled up into a tight knot at the crown of her head, to further the makeshift disguise and to avoid leaving any telltale hairs behind. She'd come to appreciate the uniqueness of both the color and curls. But tonight her distinctive hair was a nuisance.

She turned her attention to her lock picking.

It took her less than thirty seconds to get the

door to the morgue open. The room was very dim, the only light coming from one fluorescent ceiling fixture in the far corner. A couple of new residents had arrived since she'd been here last, and Alex made a silent apology as she intruded.

One of the gurneys held an elderly woman who was partially uncovered, the cloth over her lined face having slipped off. Alex hesitated, then gently pulled the cover back up. She might not have bothered before, but the harsh reality of death was weighing heavily on her, and she couldn't help thinking about the loved ones who no doubt would still grieve even though this soul's suffering had ended.

She suppressed a shiver and began to walk toward cold storage. A separate small room in the back of the morgue, it was where bodies were kept when the paperwork was complete, before they were picked up by a mortician. Oddly, the door wasn't secured. In fact, it stood slightly ajar, and she frowned. She could feel the cool air escaping through the gap.

A slight noise followed by a barely audible muttering came from the room. She froze in her tracks. If she'd been given to horror stories, a thousand possibilities would have raced into her mind. But she glimpsed something through the narrow gap between the door and the jamb that catapulted what she'd heard into an entirely new category. A narrow beam of light, moving.

A flashlight.

The room was pitch black. Anyone who belonged there would have turned on the overhead lights. And they wouldn't worry about making noise. The furtive implications of that flashlight and the effort to stay quiet started the flood of adrenaline in Alex.

She crept forward, her body instantly in the high state of alert and muscle tension that allowed her to make every careful movement utterly silent. She'd come prepared, wearing soft, leather-soled shoes rather than her running shoes with soles that could squeak too easily on the polished vinyl floors.

She peeked through the gap, saw a dark figure moving in the back of the room. The beam of the flashlight was small and intense, a xenon bulb, most likely.

The angle of the beam told her the person was tall. But it didn't reflect enough light back at its holder to enable her to see anything other than short hair and a strong build. That, coupled with something about the way he held himself, added up to her assumption of gender.

What the faint light did show her, with shocking clarity, was what the person was doing. He had opened the drawer that held Rainy's body. The sight made her stomach roil.

She must have made a sound, although she wasn't aware of anything but the outrage that filled her as she pushed open the door. The man whipped around. Instantly he aimed the high intensity flashlight at her face, blinding her and preventing her from getting a look at him. That single action told her the guy knew what he was doing. Instinctively she backed up into the morgue.

He came at her.

She took what little she knew—he was tall—and used it. She crouched. Leaped forward. Caught him just below the knees. Used the muscles of her legs to drive forward and up. Felt the moment when she had him. Flipped him.

He was back on his feet fast. Came at her again. She knew he'd be ready for her this time. But he might not expect the same thing twice. She had a split second to decide. She went for it. This time she didn't get the right angle and he flew awkwardly sideways as she rushed past him.

Still in motion she reached a counter and hit it with her right hand. Used it as a platform to spin and launch a side kick at his chest. A kick that Rainy—a tae kwon do black belt and instructor—would have been proud of. Caught him dead center and sent him reeling backward.

She landed on the balls of her feet, ready to strike in any direction. Yet the man hesitated. He'd slid into the main door to the hallway in his sprawl, and it had opened behind him, offering escape. It kept him backlit, and she was still unable to see his face.

She took a step toward him.

He pulled the gurney with the old woman forward until it was between them, then darted out the door. By the time she dodged around and reached the hallway, he was gone. She looked quickly up and down the hall but there was no sign, no doors just closing, no elevator just heading upstairs.

And I never saw his face, damn it.

She had no idea who he was, what he wanted with Rainy, if he was acting alone or if someone had sent him. Had no idea what he would have done had she not come along. She knew only that he hadn't been anyone with official authorization, from either hospital or police or family. That alone would have told her that there was more to Rainy's death than a simple accident.

But there was another layer of weirdness to this painful situation, a layer that had driven Alex back to the morgue in the middle of this hot August Sunday night for another look at her friend's body.

Copies of Rainy's medical forms from Athena Academy, which Christine Evans had e-mailed to Alex that afternoon, clearly stated that an emergency appendectomy had been performed on Rainy when she was fourteen. Alex had already known this, because when she'd been stricken with appendicitis herself in her junior year, Rainy had reassured her that all would be well, citing her own experience and showing off her scar.

And that made this situation all the more impossible.

What Alex had wanted to see again, what she hadn't been able to study and make sense of during the autopsy, were other scars that Rainy had never mentioned. Scars on her ovaries.

Because the woman on that table in the morgue had a scar in approximately the right place for an appendectomy.

And a perfectly healthy appendix.

"And you didn't recognize him? Sometimes family members go a little crazy in times of grief."

The hospital's night security supervisor, a middle-age black man with kind eyes, spoke to her gently. Alex wondered if he was implying she had also gone a little crazy, but he seemed so sincere she chose not to believe it. You had to draw the line somewhere or you'd end up hating every human being in the world.

"No, I didn't," she repeated for at least the fifth time. He was the third person she'd told the story to in the past two hours. "It all happened very fast and he came out of a dark room, but it was no one I knew. Besides," she pointed out, "if he had been a family member or friend, he would have recognized me."

She hadn't told him the whole story, didn't want to deal with the questions that would arise if he knew she'd also been inside the room and had in fact been involved in very brief hand-to-hand combat with the man. So she'd told him she'd been unable to sleep and had come to see if there was anyone here who could let her in for a last good-bye. She'd found the door unlocked—okay, so she didn't specify which door, but she didn't want to have to explain how she'd gotten in—and once inside had encountered a man who seemed to be sneaking around the back room with a flashlight.

The security man seemed to accept her implication that the man had left the outer door open. At least, as much as he was accepting any of her story. She didn't care as long as he took some action. Her main concern was to have the area secured until she could get Rainy out of there.

"Hmm." The security man rubbed his chin thoughtfully. "Your friend who died, was she FBI, too?"

"No. She's an—she was an attorney, in Tucson."

He noticed her stumble on the change in tense and seemed to reach a decision. Thankfully, it was the decision she had wanted.

"I've got a couple of hours of paperwork to do this morning before the end of my shift. I'll just grab myself a chair and do it sitting down here. That give you enough time to make your arrangements?"

"It should." Alex smiled at him gratefully. "Thank you. Thank you very much. I really appreciate this."

He didn't mention calling the sheriff's office, and she was glad of that even though it suggested he still didn't quite believe there was reason for alarm. Alex knew she was already on thin ice here. Only professional courtesy, the fact that police lieutenant Kayla Ryan had requested it and a fierce, stubborn insistence on her part had enabled her to sit in on Rainy's autopsy that morning in the first place.

They'd cut her some slack because she was FBI, but it wouldn't take much more to wear out her welcome. It never took a whole lot to wear out a fed's welcome with city, county or even state law enforcement. And pointing out that they were all supposed to be on the same side never seemed to help much.

The local authorities hadn't been enthused about the autopsy in the first place. They had clearly already resolved the case in their minds.

Rainy had fallen asleep at the wheel just outside Eloy, then gone off the road and crashed into a pole. Period. There was nothing left but the loose ends to tie up. That was the way the official report read, and that was what the investigating officers believed.

Alex knew the autopsy had been done because there were no apparent reasons for the accident. She guessed that the officers suspected Rainy had been drunk or on something illegal.

As if.

Alex had the sudden thought that she herself had sometimes dismissed the claims of family and friends about their loved ones.

In the lab, she let the fascination of the scientific process keep the reality of death at a safe distance. The fact that she was in the trace evidence department and dealt mostly with hair, fibers, paint, blood, glass and other things added to that buffer.

When the evidence pointed strongly one way, sometimes you did have to go with the numbers, simply because you had nothing else to base a decision on. If the odds were high in one direction, it took a lot of solid evidence to counter them.

And that was evidence they didn't yet have for Rainy.

"Yet" being the operative word there, she told herself, shoring up her determination.

But she was going to have to tread very carefully. Those local authorities had also made it clear what they thought of her getting any more involved because of her personal relationship with the deceased.

The deceased.

That's what Rainy was to the officials. All she was. Just another fatality case. Already death was stealing away Rainy's identity, stealing away the essence of who and what she was. These people here, making these decisions, had never known the brilliant, beautiful, generous woman she'd been. The woman who by sheer force of personality had changed six young lives and touched countless others, and who would never have tolerated being referred to in such an impersonal manner.

But Alex had known her. And loved her. And she'd be damned if she'd let anyone reduce Rainy to a case number, a statistic, just another nameless driver falling asleep at the wheel. There was more to this than that, much more. Her gut was screaming that there was, and she'd learned to trust it, whether in the lab or in life.

The problem was, her gut feelings and what little strange evidence she had led to Athena Academy. And Alex wasn't about to draw any attention to the school unless there was no choice. For now, the team name the Cassandras had chosen all those years ago would have an ironic significance—they were all feeling there was more to Rainy's demise than the official determination of "accidental death," yet, like the prophetess of old, they could get no one to believe them.

As she waited for the security man to return with the mentioned chair, Alex retrieved the smock she'd hastily stuffed into the trash can just down the hall after calling in the intruder to security. There was a laundry cart standing unattended outside another door, and she ran down and stuffed the disguise into the soiled linens bag.

By the time the security supervisor came back she was standing back where she'd been, looking as if she'd been there all the time. In addition to the chair, he carried a large clipboard with a stack of forms on it, so he'd clearly been truthful about settling in to do paperwork.

She thanked him again, clasping his hand in hers, and told him she'd let him know as soon as arrangements were made to move Rainy. Then she headed quickly toward the elevators. It took her a few minutes to find a place at the hospital where she was both allowed to use her cell phone and able to get a signal. She ended up back at the main front doors, and even then she had to walk out from under the huge cement quadrangle-shaped portico that marked the entrance.

It was just after 6:00 a.m., but she didn't hesitate in dialing Kayla Ryan's cell phone.

She felt a strange sense of both familiarity and oddness as she made the call. There had been a time when she would have called her old Athena classmate anytime there was something bursting out of her that she simply had to talk about. But that closeness had disappeared a long time ago, and the chasm that had opened between them over Kayla's affair with Mike Bridges, the cocky young officer who had fathered Kayla's daughter and then deserted them both, had never quite healed.

But none of that ancient history mattered now. The Cassandra promise had been invoked. Every one of them would live up to the promise, and they would all pull together as if the years since they'd left Athena Academy had never existed.

Kayla answered on the first ring.

"It's Alex." She wasted no time on preamble. "An intruder was in the morgue at the hospital. He was trying to do something to or with Rainy."

She heard Kayla suck in a breath, could imagine the change in her expression as she snapped into police mode. "Any idea who?"

"No. Didn't get a look at him at all. He was tall, in good shape. He was good, maybe a pro. Probably covered his tracks well. But I'm not even sure what he was going to do. I interrupted him just as he was…reaching for her."

She bit her lip. Hard. Tasted blood. Didn't

care. God, this hurt so much, to even think that the cold, lifeless body in a drawer was really, truly Rainy. Or at least all that was left of her in this world.

"We've got to get her out of there and back on Athena turf," Kayla said, with a briskness Alex guessed hid feelings similar to her own. Kayla had also voiced her own first choice; she'd feel much better when Rainy was out of the hands of strangers who didn't know who they had, how special she was, that she was worth any effort.

"Yes. To the morgue there in Athens, preferably," Alex said, referring to the small town adjacent to the academy. On the map Athens was a continuation of the Phoenix sprawl, but in fact had grown up into a town of about five thousand as an adjunct to the academy, housing many of the staff and support services, and suppliers to the school.

It was also Kayla's jurisdiction.

Kayla quickly picked up on her inference. "You want her there, not just to a mortuary?"

"Exactly. I want her where we can have someone we know and trust take a closer look. This doctor's good, but he's not a coroner or an investigator. The county doesn't have one, they have to borrow from the next county over, and they won't do it unless they're really suspicious."

"And they're not," Kayla said.

"No. They're already convinced it was just an accident, that she fell asleep."

"As if," Kayla muttered, and Alex's mouth

quirked at the perfect repetition of her own response, even as she felt a qualm that she and this woman she had once been so close to had become so estranged. Kayla's next words wiped all levity from her mind.

"I was going to call you this morning. Your guy isn't the first intruder. Someone was inside Rainy and Marshall's house yesterday." Kayla explained that the person had run and Kayla hadn't gotten a look at him. Or her. "I also checked out Rainy's car at the county forensics lab. The seat belt failed."

Alex sucked in a breath. "Any sign of tampering?"

"None. What are the odds." Her tone was grim.

"We should move her today."

"I'll make the arrangements with Marshall," Kayla said.

"How is he?" Alex asked. Then felt foolish. Rainy had been their friend but Marshall Carrington's wife, so how did she think he was?

"He's…handling it," Kayla said.

Alex wasn't sure what that meant, or what the odd note in Kayla's voice indicated, but she didn't have time to delve into extraneous details now.

"Will he agree to move her?"

"I think so. I'll make the arrangements from here, and I'll call you as soon as it's done."

"Good."

"Listen, Alex…there's something else that might play into this."

"What?"

"Marshall said Rainy had been undergoing fertility treatments. He told me that her doctor said she might not be able to conceive because of scarring on her ovaries."

Alex instantly went on full alert. She'd called Kayla after the autopsy to tell her about Rainy's appendix and the scars, but hadn't mentioned any of her vague suspicions. "Oh?"

"Yes. Apparently Dr. Halburg, Rainy's gynecologist, said the scarring was natural. And not uncommon, even."

"Hmm." Alex frowned. "Did he say if they were trying for in vitro?"

"I didn't get to ask. That's when we realized someone was in the house. But there was information on egg mining in Rainy's office."

"Maybe it's nothing more than that, then." Alex said it, but she didn't believe it. Not with two intruders in the same twelve-hour period. Or perhaps it was the same person.

"You'll be headed to Athens, then?" Kayla asked.

"Yes. I'll follow the transport to the morgue, just to be sure." She made a mental note to call work and extend her personal leave, as well.

"Will you be staying on the grounds at Athena? Do you want me to call Christine?"

"No, I'll get her on my cell when I'm on my way," Alex said.

Athena's principal was getting ready for the arrival of students for the next trimester starting on the first of September, but Christine Evans lived by the philosophy "Once an Athena woman, always an Athena woman," and all the graduates were like family to her. And she'd been especially close to Rainy, so Alex knew she'd do anything necessary to help find the truth about her death.

"I've got an investigation that's got to be tied up," Kayla was saying, "but I'll check in with you and get to Athena when I can. I'll see when my sister can watch Jazz."

"How is she?" Alex asked, embarrassedly aware that this was the first time she'd asked. Kayla's eleven-year-old daughter, Jasmine, was one positive thing that had come out of Kayla's youthful fling. The girl was bright and pretty, looking much more like her honey-skinned mother than what Alex remembered of her father.

"She's the light of my life," Kayla said simply, and quickly went on. "I'll be in touch when arrangements are made to move Rainy."

Alex felt the sting of the quick subject change.

"All right," she said, realizing this was not the time or place to go into things like their personal situation.

There was an awkward moment of silence between them, a moment that would have once been impossible between the two who had been the closest of friends. On the heels of the sting, Alex felt a moment of the old irritation at the fact that this estrangement was over, of all things, a man.

A boy, really, she amended silently. Mike had been a shallow charmer with zero sense of responsibility. And still was, most likely. But Kayla had

thought herself in love, and had thrown her childhood away for it.

Just goes to show, Alex thought, even Athena
Academy can't break all of women's stupid habits.

Chapter 2

The stark difference between this time and all the other times Alex had traveled the road from Phoenix to Athena tore at the very core of her. Before, she had always approached this passage with joy, anticipating the turn onto Olympus Road, knowing that soon after she'd reach Script Pass, the road to Athena, all the while eagerly awaiting another new year of school. But now...

She shook her head, trying to clear it as she drove behind the black van that was serving as a hearse for Rainy's body. She knew she was tired, she'd been up nearly all night, but adrenaline was still pumping and she knew from past experience just how far it would carry her. She was all right for a while yet.

Once she was through the Phoenix metro area, Alex slipped her headset over her right ear and hit the speed dial number on her cell for Christine Evans at Athena. Christine answered on the second ring. Alex gave her only the essentials over the cell connection. She was bringing Rainy home, and would need a place to stay for a while.

"Of course," Christine said instantly. "Everything's open until the first, including your old dorm if you want it. After that you can stay with me, or in one of the guest houses. We won't have any families or guests visiting for the first month."

Alex knew that was standard, to give new students time to settle in to the school routine without interruption. Those 6:30 a.m. reveilles were a shock for some students, as the hot, dry climate was for others, and the acclimatization to both took time.

"That's fine. I'll figure that out when I get there."

"Which will be?"

"I just cleared the Phoenix city limits, so I'm about a half hour out. But I'll be…securing things at the morgue in Athens first."

The former army captain didn't miss the inference. She also didn't make the mistake of pursuing it in a cell conversation that could be monitored. "I see. I should expect you in the early evening, then?"

"Probably. I'll call you."

"All right." There was a pause. "Alex?"

"Yes?"

"It will be good to spend time with you. I just wish the circumstances were different."

"No more than I," Alex said fervently.

After the call Alex tried to think of other things. Of how strange this place had seemed to her east-coast eyes the first time she'd come here. Used to the rolling green hills of northern Virginia and the time-worn mountains of the east coast, she'd found the dry desert flatness and jagged peaks as strange as any moonscape.

She'd initially wondered why on earth they'd located the school here, when they'd had the entire country to choose from. She'd even asked her grandfather, Charles Forsythe, one of the founders and main backers of Athena, why they'd picked that spot. And had asked it, she'd much later realized, with all the arrogance of a teenager who was certain she knew it all.

He'd told her that they'd chosen this place for all the reasons she thought it was a bad choice. She hadn't understood then, but eventually she'd realized the wisdom of the selection.

And she had come to love it for its own kind of stark, harsh beauty, and to respect it for what it had to teach the women of Athena about reality and survival and the incontrovertible facts of nature and life. It had become their sanctuary even as it was their proving ground. Being dropped in the wilds of the White Tank Mountains with minimal supplies and told to find your way back had a way of teaching you a new perspective.

But she doubted there was any perspective to be gained in this case. There had been no one in her life quite like Rainy. And there never would be again. There had been only five years age difference between them, but at times Rainy had seemed as much a mother figure as an older sister. Perhaps, Alex had thought more than once, because her own mother had been so cool and distant.

She'd felt closer to Rainy than even her own blood sibling. She loved her big brother, Bennington, dearly, but he also had the knack of irritating the heck out of her more than anyone else ever could. In fact, she'd felt closer to Rainy than any of her family except her grandfather Charles, or G.C., as she'd called him since childhood. It was a nickname her mother had despised, which of course had guaranteed Alex would use it as often as possible.

Alex reached over to the passenger seat and grabbed the bottle of spring water she'd tucked inside the large shoulder bag she used as both purse and briefcase. And holster, if it came to that. The bag had a special outside-access pocket for her duty weapon concealed between the two divided sections.

She took a long drink, knowing that keeping hydrated in this desert climate was crucial. She'd been gone long enough to have lost some of her adaptive abilities to this kind of arid heat; Washington D.C. was beyond hot in the summer, but arid was not a frequently used adjective there. She was thankful the new FBI crime lab was in Quantico; the proximity to the Potomac gave a bit of relief when the capital itself was sweltering.

The black van in front of her changed lanes to go around a slow-moving truck, and Alex had to wait for a break between vehicles to follow. There hadn't been this much traffic when she'd attended Athena, either, she thought. She'd graduated just thirteen years ago, but the roads between Phoenix and Athens had been a lot emptier then. Traffic would thin out the closer she got, but still, there was a marked difference.

Not for the first time she was grateful to the people, including her grandfather, who had had the vision for Athena. The late Arizona senator Marion Gracelyn had begun it, and it had evolved from her initial idea of a military-type academy just for women into the much bigger, more far-reaching thing it was now, an institution dedicated to helping women take their rightful place in a world that was still very much run by men.

When she'd first arrived, after the trek through a strange land to a strange place, she'd been wondering why she'd worked so hard to come here. She'd known it was expected of her, the Forsythe fortune having helped found the school. But as seventh grade and the time to go to the school she hadn't chosen neared, she had rebelled against this set future even as it closed in on her, purposely refusing to do her schoolwork and messing around during national testing. Only the awful disappointment of her beloved grandfather had shaken her off her mutinous course and sent her back to work.

As it was, she'd lost a year and had come to Athena as an eighth grader. She'd been assigned an orientation group with seventh-grade girls who would become the Cassandras. The age difference had made for problems in itself, but Rainy had straightened that out as she had straightened them all out.

She had been the force that had brought them together, had taken the young girls they had been and transformed them into a cohesive unit of smart, capable, skilled women who could handle anything thrown their way.

Alex blinked rapidly as tears blurred her vision. This was impossible. It just could not be happening. She could not be driving back to Athena behind a van carrying Rainy's body.

Her cell phone rang, startling her. She'd forgotten it was still in her lap. She glanced at the caller ID, considered letting it go to voice mail, then chided herself for being a coward. She flipped the phone open.

"Hello, Emerson."

"Alexandra."

Emerson Howland, Alex's fiancé, was the only person on the planet besides her mother who called her that. Even her grandfather called her Alex. Emerson's manner sometimes made her feel as if the age gap between them was even greater than twelve years. But he had told her once he thought

Alexandra a lovely name, so she'd finally given up trying to break him of the habit. She admired so much about him—the man's work was, after all, saving others—that it seemed a petty thing to nag him about.

She waited for him to speak. He seemed to be waiting for her to do the same. She was never sure if it was some kind of power thing on his end, or simply that generation's deep, inbred, sometimes cool politeness that marked his every interaction.

She found she was in no mood for that, either. "You called me," she pointed out.

There was a pause, just long enough for her to consider how snippy she'd sounded. But before she could say anything, he spoke again.

"Your mother says hello."

"Oh?"

She stopped herself from pointing out that her mother had her number if she wanted to say hello. Not likely, she knew. Odd, when her own mother would rather speak to Alex's fiancé than her. But then, her upper-crust mother highly approved of Emerson. In fact, she usually seemed happier to see him than her own daughter on those occasions they were together—which came as infrequently as Alex could manage.

"Yes, I dropped some flowers off at the house today. For her birthday."

Drat. I forgot. I'll have to send something. Fast.

"That was thoughtful," she said into the phone. "I'm sure she appreciated it."

Funny how he remembered her mother's birthday, and her mother remembered his, while the woman could barely bestir herself to remember her own daughter's. But if that daughter forgot hers…

"She mentioned she hadn't heard from you." He paused, but she said nothing. She had long ago stopped responding to her mother's guilt-laden efforts at what she called communication. "So…how are you?" This time he sounded as if he really wanted to know.

"About like you'd expect."

"I am sorry, Alexandra. I know she was a dear friend."

She felt bad about her snappishness. "Thank you, Emerson. I'm just a little edgy."

"I should go. I have a meeting."

"The triple valve replacement?" she asked, expressing an interest she didn't really feel.

"Yes. The surgery is scheduled for Tuesday. We're optimistic about the final result."

She was certain he had reason to be. Emerson was one of the premier cardiac surgeons in the country, and his skill in saving lives and his willingness to travel anywhere to do it were two of the things she loved about him.

"Good luck, then."

There was an awkward moment of silence followed by perfunctory goodbyes. They had never done that very well, as if each of them felt there should be more said but neither knew what it was.

She let out a breath she hadn't realized she

was holding. Relationships were so much more complex then the trails of evidence she loved to analyze, dissect and follow to an inarguable conclusion.

She thought about what she'd seen in the cold storage room when she'd gone back in to look at the scene and resecure Rainy before she'd contacted anyone about the intruder. She'd found no trace evidence, and hadn't had the means to check for fingerprints. But there had been a gurney near Rainy's body. And on that gurney an empty black body bag.

And she wondered if his plan hadn't been to tamper with Rainy's body, but to steal it.

Alex didn't protest when Christine pressed a glass of wine into her hands. She knew she was on edge, now that she was here and the task at hand had been accomplished. Rainy's body was secured in Athens's small morgue and was being watched over by an off-duty officer hand-selected by Kayla. Alex had forced herself to leave and get some food and rest, knowing she was in no shape to act or think clearly in any technical area.

Besides, the doctor Christine had called in would not be available until tomorrow. So, in the morning she would head to the morgue and get her questions answered. Those that had answers, anyway.

Alex looked at the woman who had been the heart and soul of Athena for over two decades. Christine had built the crucial part of Athena from the beginning, had searched out and handpicked the staff of instructors, carefully assessing each for not just their intelligence and aptitude for teaching, but for their ability to understand and dedicate themselves to Athena's cause.

It was that last that had eliminated more candidates than anything else. Not everyone had the mind-set to work for the most state-of-the-art college-prep school for women in the country. When you threw in some of the more controversial subjects in the program of study, it made the selection process even more delicate. Not everyone agreed with Athena's stated goal, the empowerment of women in America. In all areas. It was Christine's job to weed out those who couldn't come to Athena with the wholehearted desire to make it possible for her students to achieve what was now so difficult simply because they were women.

Christine also made the final choices of the students, selecting only the best and brightest in both academics and athletics. Those few who met her standards were sent invitations to attend Athena Academy. In fact, a stack of folders was on the coffee table in front of her, and Alex knew Christine was going through them, familiarizing herself with each of the thirty or so new students who would be entering the academy. She was careful to welcome each new arrival by name when she first saw them. Athena, she always said, was an intimidating place, and she wanted to be sure each girl knew she was expected and wanted. That it was not simply that the student was lucky to be here, but also that Athena was lucky to have her.

And Alex was just rattled enough tonight to ask something that had been living in the back of her mind for years, ever since she had realized how truly hard one of those invitations was to get.

"Why did I get asked to Athena?"

Christine blinked. She turned her head slightly, as she did when she wanted to study something or someone carefully. She'd been blinded in her left eye in a training exercise, which had resulted in her retirement from military service. But it was also why she'd ended up running Athena, so she'd often said she had no complaints. Even at sixty-one she could still keep up with most of the rigorous training at Athena, and she ran the weaponry, horsemanship and survival courses herself. She even taught Arabic.

"You were asked," Christine said after a moment, "because you deserved to be asked."

"It wasn't because of my grandfather?"

Christine leaned back in her chair. She took a sip from her own glass of wine. "You know what Athena is all about. Do you really think we support nepotism? That we would take someone who didn't qualify simply because they had a relative who is on the board?"

"No," Alex admitted. "I know the school takes nothing with any strings attached. But—"

"And even if we did," Christine went on as if she

hadn't spoken, "no one graduates here without having earned it. Fully and completely."

"But you go by federal and state test scores, and mine had plummeted," Alex said. "My whole average, in everything, took a big hit the year before I came to Athena."

"We only begin the selection process with those scores," Christine corrected her mildly. "And, independently of your grandfather, you had come to our attention long before that year when you decided to resist."

Alex colored slightly. Christine smiled.

"Did you think you were the only rebel we ever took on? The only one who purposely messed up, just to spoil everyone's expectations?"

Alex shook her head, feeling a bit sheepish. "I guess I didn't think about it at all."

"And you," Christine said, gesturing toward Alex with her glass, "had the highest set of expectations imaginable placed on you, with your grandfather being a founder, on the board and a primary financial backer of Athena."

"It was just that nobody asked *me* what I wanted to do," she said, suddenly feeling compelled to explain that year of rebellion when she'd refused to work at all. "It was like it was a given I'd come to Athena, whether I wanted to or not." She grimaced. "So I set out to make that impossible, just to show them."

It was the only time in her life she'd intentionally done something she knew would hurt or disappoint her grandfather. And although he'd gently forgiven her and told her he understood, she still regretted it.

"We know how to look beyond rebellion," Christine said. "In fact, we often look *for* it. A strong spirit and will are also essential here." Then, in a seeming non sequitur, Christine asked, "How is Emerson?"

Alex blinked. "Fine, I suppose. I talked to him earlier today."

If Christine thought it odd that she hadn't mentioned the man she was supposed to marry since she'd arrived, it didn't show in her face. And Alex wondered if there had been a point to this seeming change of subject, if Christine was implying that Emerson and a woman of strong spirit and will were a questionable match. The woman had met Emerson once, when she'd made a trip to D.C. and they had gotten together for dinner and introductions. But Christine was better than anyone Alex had ever known, inside the FBI or out, at sizing people up quickly. And she was rarely wrong.

Christine studied Alex for a moment, her expression softening. When she spoke, it was on the previous subject. "Do you regret giving in?"

Alex drew back sharply. "And coming to Athena? Of course not!"

"You seemed to, at first. I know you had a hard time, being older than the other Cassandras."

"I was a pain in the butt," Alex said bluntly. "I know everyone thought I was snooty and aloof be-

cause of my background, because I was a Forsythe, but really I was just…ambivalent about the
whole thing."

"And now?"

"Athena was the best thing that ever happened
to me. I wouldn't trade coming here, and what I
learned here, for anything."

Her voice had grown rather fierce, and it made
Christine smile. "We're changing the world, Alex.
Slowly, but with each graduating class, we're
showing humankind just how much women are
capable of, given the same training and opportunities men have."

Alex thought about what Christine had said
later, as she lay in bed. She was in the guest house
closest to the mountains, which she had picked for
its relative isolation. She'd originally intended to
sleep in her old dorm room, but the memories were
far too strong there, the hole left by Rainy's death
too ragged and fresh for her to stay. It was in that
room that they'd made the Cassandra promise, the
pledge to come if any of the others needed them,
no questions asked.

We're changing the world…

She rolled onto her side, punching a hollow for
her head in the pillow. Were they? Really? It didn't
seem that way sometimes. The man she'd encountered in the morgue seemed living proof of that.
But Josie Lockworth, a fellow Cassandra, had always said they had to look at the bigger picture.

Alex had valued Josie's words because she felt that Josie could really relate to her background, Josie's father having been both a supporter of the building of Athena and not coincidentally the director of the CIA at the time. Alex supposed that butting her head against that thickest of glass ceilings, that of the military establishment, had made Josie more aware that changes like this took not years but decades, generations.

She changed to her other side, kicking off the sheet and thin blanket.

Maybe that's what they were doing, she thought. Changing the long-term, bigger picture. Each woman they put in a position denied to women before meant a younger generation of men and women grew up with the idea that it was normal. Which cleared the way to the next step. And then the next.

Alex sat up with a disgusted sigh. She'd expected to be asleep before she had time to think about anything, especially after being up since two that morning and having a full meal and a glass of wine. But here she was, wide-awake, unable to shut off her mind.

Never one to resort to chemical sleep aids, she rolled out of bed and dressed in jeans, running shoes and a white knit tank top. At night, at least, she didn't have to pour sunscreen on the pale skin that went with her hair.

She stepped outside, the shock of heat hitting her. In D.C., it got hot, seemed hotter because of the humidity, but it generally cooled off at least some at night. Here, at this time of year, it wasn't unusual to be out at 2:00 a.m. in temperatures near ninety. Fortunately it wasn't that hot now, but it was still enough to bring on memories of hot summer nights at Athena.

She needed no flashlight. She knew these grounds as well as she knew her house in Alexandria, a D.C. suburb. Off to her right she saw lights on in Christine's bungalow, where Christine was no doubt still working in preparation for the incoming students. To her left was the library, and in front of that, beyond the parking lot, was the dorm building she'd avoided tonight.

She stopped walking and looked at the two-story building that had once been a spa of the sort that rich people who had picked up certain addictions went to for treatment. It had been converted into an efficient and pleasant, if no longer quite so luxurious, fifty-room dormitory.

She turned and looked up at the mountains behind her, at the view she'd had from her dorm room's balcony for her entire stay at Athena. More than once she'd slept out there so that she could wake to see the first rays of the sun paint the stark landscape that had once been so strange to her.

She made her way past the library to the science labs, then wandered toward the main building that housed the classrooms, offices and auditorium. She'd been awed by the options presented at Athena, at the chances to study things never offered in a regular school—the local high school didn't run to martial arts, cryptology, weapons and criminal profiling in addition to lock picking, nor did they encourage students to intern with the FBI, CIA or other agency of choice.

Moved by an emotion born of her discussion with Christine and her thoughts afterward, she walked to the front entrance of the school. She went on to Script Pass, the only road that led to Athena. She turned and looked back, past the fountain and flowers at the center of the circular drive, over the lawn in front of the main building, up to the dark shapes of the mountains beyond. In the moonlight it all had an ethereal silver glow.

It was almost as ethereal in the public eye. The founders had decided from the beginning to keep Athena low profile. Their goal was not glory for the school, but for its students. And invitation-only institutions were subject to too much speculation and self-righteous curiosity, especially when it came to those that were funded the way Athena was. The students were not encouraged to discuss their alma mater with outsiders, but in educational circles and beyond, the sheer and consistent excellence of the Athena graduates was beginning to create a stir.

Most people have never heard of us, but we *are* changing the world, Alex thought.

In a burst of nostalgia, she headed back onto the school grounds, her goal the stables. She and her horse Lacy had spent many a long hour exploring those mountains. She'd honed Lacy's condition in the White Tank Mountain Regional Park. Now twenty years old, Lacy—registered under the name of Chantilly Lace, a tradition with Forsythe horses since the family fortune had been founded on rich fabrics centuries ago—was living a well-earned retirement on her grandfather's Virginia ranch, nothing more pressing to do than graze on the rich grass. But several of Lacy's offspring were here, contributing to the versatility of Athena students just as the mare had.

Alex was past the admin office when she felt the tickle at the back of her neck.

Chapter 3

She was being followed.

She knew her hair alone made her quite recognizable, even in just the moonlight. Red, curly manes like hers weren't that common. So it followed that if it were Christine, or one of the other staff who knew she was there, they would call out to her.

She picked up her pace without appearing to hurry, merely lengthening her stride. So did the person behind her, although he—or she—kept to the shadows to stay hidden. And if Alex's nerves hadn't been so ragged, the ploy might have succeeded; whoever it was was good. Very good.

Trained.

That was the word to come into her mind, and she'd learned to go with gut feelings like that, because most of the time they were right. The man from the cold storage room in the morgue? That, she couldn't tell.

She veered to the right, toward the riding arena. The open area left little cover for her follower. It also made Alex's path quite visible in the moonlight, so whoever it was could see her direction without having to leave cover. It was clear he—she became fairly certain of her shadow's gender as she watched the way he moved—was following her.

The question of why was looming, but she didn't waste time on it. More important right now was the question of his capabilities. Trained could easily mean armed. But she'd already given him ample chance to try to take her out that way if that was his goal.

So if that wasn't his goal, what was? Was he after someone else? Something else?

Alex changed course again, heading once more toward her original goal, the stables. She stepped inside. Her pursuer hung back, waiting, she guessed, to see if she emerged. She checked the door of the always lit up stable office. Locked. Did she have time to break in and use the phone? She could probably find something to use on the lock, but she would lose track of her stalker. She risked a look out the tack room window that faced back the way she had come.

After a moment she saw the slightest movement in the shadow of the science lab building. An even darker shadow. It moved again, barely, and she saw the slightest glint of moonlight on metal.

A gun?

It had been in the right place for a waistband holster. If she was right, he was indeed armed. She was not.

She darted out of the tack room, whispered an acknowledgement to the horses who nickered a greeting, then raced up the ladder to the hayloft with all the speed of the fourteen-year-old she'd once been. From there she could see clearly both where her follower was hiding and the path to the staff bungalows. She settled in to see what the man would do.

He waited.

Patient, she thought. But was he waiting until he was sure the coast was clear to make a move, or waiting for her to emerge?

She could be just as patient. They'd taught that at Athena, too.

She waited. And so did he. Minutes ticked away. She wished she'd brought her cell phone, she could call Christine and warn her there was someone skulking around. She wondered who would break first.

And with a sigh, she knew. She would. Because while Athena had taught her patience, it had also taught her about the benefits of taking action, striking first, of bringing the game to your own court and on your own terms.

Athena was her court. No one except another

Athenan could know it as well as she did. She would use that. And whatever else came to hand.

Alex crept back to the tack room. Amid the hanging saddles, bridles and blankets, she found an old hunt coat. It was obviously due for retirement, more than a little threadbare, but it was dark and hid the white shirt that glowed like neon in the moonlight.

She harvested a bonus out of the right pocket, a large, dark blue bandanna. In a few seconds she had the red-gold beacon of her hair bundled up and covered. She searched around for additional trimmings and found a pair of rubber knee-high muck-out boots. They were large enough to slide on over her shoes. There was a mirror in the tack room, and she checked out the look. With luck, it would pass.

She went back to the door. She took a couple of deep breaths. Little steps, she thought. The boots would help, they were big enough that she'd have to alter her stride anyway. She purposely slumped her shoulders, as she'd seen women do who weren't comfortable with their height. She bent her knees slightly, as far as she thought she could without it being obvious from a distance, to make herself seem shorter. She changed everything she'd been taught to watch for to see through disguises in her own training.

If the man was trained as she thought he was, he wouldn't miss the marked differences beyond simple appearance. She just had to hope he wouldn't look close enough to see through her ruse.

She stepped out of the stable through the same door she'd entered, figuring he'd be watching where she'd gone in. When she was in full moonlight, she turned back and waved at the doorway.

"See ya tomorrow!" she called out cheerfully, raising the pitch of her natural voice and injecting just the slightest bit of a drawl.

She set off toward the staff housing, humming a light, cheerful tune. But every bit of her awareness and concentration was focused on the perimeter of the science lab building. She caught the faintest glint as moonlight reflected on what she still suspected was a gun. Then she made out a slightly darker shadow within the shadow. He moved, she thought. No, turned. Just turned to watch her. Made no move to follow her. And after a moment, she saw the glint again, as he turned back and resumed his scrutiny of the stables, clearly indicating his lack of interest in this "second" woman.

So he is following me, specifically, Alex thought. She could handle that. At least the guy wasn't after Christine. Although even if he was, he'd find he had his hands more full than he might have expected, especially if he judged her only by her age. Athenan women didn't just age gracefully, they aged tough.

She took advantage of the fact that he'd returned his attention to the stables. She dodged behind the school's large, four-horse trailer, parked beside the stable. From where he was, he shouldn't be able to see beneath it all the way, and so couldn't see her feet. Since it had living quarters at the front, it was nearly thirty-five feet long and covered her retreat back to the stables. Keeping the trailer between her and the man watching, she made her way to the back side of the stable, out of sight. She went over the fence, through an outside stall door and back into the building, whispering soothingly to the chestnut gelding who occupied the stall.

"Easy, sweetie. Just passing through."

She quickly went out the inner stall door. She shed the dark jacket, the boots, and freed her hair. She knew which horse she wanted, although she didn't know which stall she was in. But as if she sensed Alex's presence, the gray stuck her head over the half door. Alex hastened to greet the mare, a granddaughter of her beloved Lacy.

"There you are, gorgeous. Wanna play?"

The mare called Charm—short for Charmeuse, another in the line of Forsythe fabric names—had the same bright intelligence in her dark eyes as Lacy had. Alex had ridden the mare back on her grandfather's farm, before Charm was donated to Athena, so she knew what the horse could do. She also knew Charm had the same sensitivity, willingness and trust as her granddam. And for a gallivant such as Alex had in mind, that was what she needed.

She bridled the mare, who took the bit easily despite the oddity of the hour. Grabbing a handful of mane, Alex launched herself onto the horse's back.

She settled into place and headed the gray toward the still-open door she'd exited in her other guise. The clatter of the shod hooves on the stable floor was comfortingly familiar. In fact, it felt so good to be on a horse again, she wondered why she didn't ride more regularly. It wasn't like she had to go very far, since her grandfather's farm was only half an hour outside of D.C.

She leaned forward to pat the mare's neck. "All right, my Charm girl. Let's teach somebody a lesson about messing with Athena."

They stepped into the moonlight. Alex sat the horse casually, as if a moonlit bareback ride was what she'd had in mind all along. She reined the mare slightly toward the building where the watcher was hiding, just to make sure he got a good look. Alex sensed as much as saw a sharp movement in the shadows.

Gotcha.

She headed the horse slowly toward the trail that led into the mountains behind Athena. Then she urged the gray into the leggy canter that was like riding a rocking chair, even bareback.

She had mentally picked her spot before she'd ever started in that direction. She'd spent so many hours staring up at the mountains from the grounds that she knew exactly what could be seen from where. She cued Charm as they neared the cluster of scrubby whitethorn acacia trees. The moment they were past them she spun the gray off the trail into the soft dirt behind the trees, the perfect spot for an ambush. The mare dug in her heels and executed a stop that would have done a champion stock horse proud.

Alex leaped down and ground-tied the mare by tossing the reins over her head to dangle, all it took for the well-trained animal. She moved in a crouch to where she could look back the way they'd come. She spotted him immediately. Her lure was working, and he'd stepped out from the shadows and stood in plain sight, looking up toward the mountains.

"If I had my HK, I could take you out just like that," she whispered to herself. "Come on, follow me."

She was joking about the Heckler & Koch sniper rifle. But she took the man seriously. Whoever he was she sensed he was a threat to someone or something she held dear. And she, as any Athenan, would protect what she loved. Whatever it took.

She waited, watching, as he moved across the open land between the science lab and the stable. He stopped near the stable door and stared up the trail. Charm stood quietly, patiently, as any Athena horse was expected to do. Seconds, then minutes ticked by. Still she and her amiable companion waited and watched, Alex deriving not a little pleasure in having so completely turned the tables on their observer.

She saw him glance at the stables, and instinctively knew what he was thinking.

She almost hoped he would do it. It would be something to see, since she somehow doubted he was an experienced horseman.

Instead of getting a horse he started walking along the path she'd taken between the stable and the arena. He probably thought she had continued at full tilt up the mountain trail, and thus was long out of sight and hearing. Which had been, of course, her intent. He'd have been more on guard approaching her in the stable, but here he had no idea what her position might be.

He stopped at the foot of the mountain trail, still looking upward. She could see him a little better now, not his face, but at least that he had dark hair, was solidly built and tall.

So was the guy at the morgue in Casa Grande.

Was this him? Could she have been followed? Was he good enough to tail her without her noticing? She didn't think so, not all the way to Athena.

Another thought struck her. What if he hadn't had to follow her? What if he'd already known Athena was where she was going? Or would go?

That idea made her jaw tighten. Being followed was one thing. Having somebody know for certain where she would go, and having him also know where Athena was, indicated prior knowledge and had implications she didn't like.

She inhaled sharply when he turned and walked back to the stable. As he peered through the stable door she'd left open, she had to suppress a sudden urge to vault onto Charm's back and charge down there, yank the guy off his feet and do whatever it took to get him to talk, to tell her what he was doing here, what he was after. Patience had been a long and hard lesson for her to learn in her years here, she who had never had to wait for much in her privileged life. But like everything at Athena, the lessons—both academic and otherwise—had been tailored to the individual, and she'd been forced to learn that one, albeit sometimes the hard way.

She waited.

He stepped inside the stable.

She waited some more.

And waited.

Waited still.

After an hour, she wondered if he were simply going to stay there until she came back, stage an ambush of his own. Did he figure he could get away with it because there was so little staff here on the break between trimesters?

As she sat there she puzzled through what few facts she knew. She was fairly certain no one would be after her because of any cases she'd worked. As a Forensic Scientist II in the Trace Evidence unit, she wasn't high profile enough for that. She hadn't testified in any big cases that would bring someone down on her. Her superiors generally took care of that, even if she had done the work. She wasn't in it for the glory, so didn't care. Although if the promotion she was up for came through, that would change.

It had to be about Rainy. And if that were the

case, that left only a few possibilities she could think of. Somebody thought she knew something they didn't want her to know. Or, they were afraid she'd find something.

If she was right and this was connected to Rainy's death, it quite simply proved her theory that there was much more to this than an accident.

Suddenly she sharpened her attention, realizing her tired mind and body had been drifting. She hadn't slept, she was sure, but the sky was changing from black to inky blue. As the first glow of actual light broke in the distance, she realized she'd have to risk the gun and go down before it became too light to move surreptitiously, if she wanted to catch him. Moving quickly, running on sheer willpower, she remounted the ever-patient Charm and tried to keep the stable in sight as she headed down the trail slowly enough to stay quiet.

As it turned out, she didn't need to be quiet. She heard the throaty roar of a motorcycle break the stillness. Charm's ears snapped forward at the unaccustomed sound.

Not a machine to sneak around with, Alex thought as the sound echoed around her, but ideal for coming and going cross-country rather than by the road, which probably made it a good choice, she admitted reluctantly.

Moments later as the sound began to fade to the north, she realized he'd done exactly that.

"Okay," she muttered, "so you're a smart boy." She legged Charm into a gallop and sent her cutting across the grounds back to the stable. She entered cautiously, but the man was gone. Quickly she took care of the willing gray, crooning to her as she did a quick grooming and checked her hooves for stones. Satisfied, she double-checked the feeding instructions posted on the stall and gave the horse a small scoop of the appropriate grain mixture, not enough to interfere with her routine but enough to reward her for the extra effort of the night.

Then she set about searching the stable, both to make sure he'd left nothing behind and that he had done no damage. The horses began to nicker greetings, no doubt thinking she was there for morning feeding. She checked the stalls first, to make sure each animal was safe and unharmed. Then she went about the rest methodically, starting at one end of the building, intending to work to the other, from top to bottom. Then she stopped. Turned to look from the doorway across the stable.

He was good, she thought. She'd seen that. Likely a pro. So where would he have gone to wait? Where would she have gone? She scanned the shadowy interior, gauging. After a moment she headed for the third stall on the right.

It was empty. There was no feed and care regimen posted, so she assumed it had been vacant for a while, the straw inside waiting for a new occupant.

He'd been very careful. But she knew. Not just because the empty stall was the most logical, but because there was the faintest of flat spots in the straw near the outer door. When she got there she covered her hand with her shirt and unlatched the top half of the Dutch door, knowing she'd come back to check it for prints, though she doubted there'd be any. Then she knew she was right, because without opening it any farther, she could see straight up the trail she had taken into the foothills.

He'd watched from here. Patiently. Until the growing light had chased him away.

What he would have done if she'd come back, she had no idea. Would he have attacked? Tried to kill her? He'd had a chance at that, so she didn't think murder had been his intention. At least, not yet. But what could he have hoped to accomplish simply by watching?

Contact? Had that been the goal? And if so, why? And why her?

She had no idea and at this point was simply glad he hadn't hurt the horses in any way. She hastened out of the stall, secured the doors once more, and continued her search. When she was satisfied that he'd left nothing behind—at least, nothing that she would be able to find without some equipment she didn't have—she headed at a jog toward staff housing and the principal's bungalow.

This was not going to please Christine at all. Athena was her baby, she had dedicated herself to the school and its students completely, and she would take any threat to it very, very seriously.

"I'm taking it pretty damned seriously myself,"

Alex muttered aloud. "In fact, I'd have to say I'm downright ticked off."

Well, whoever he was, he probably hadn't gotten what he wanted. And if he came back, he would soon learn it wasn't smart to tick off a Cassandra.

Chapter 4

"You're certain you're all right?"

"Of course," Alex told her former principal. "He never got anywhere near me. Unfortunately, I didn't get near him, either."

"Mmm," Christine murmured. "And if he'd gone after someone or something else?"

"I would have stopped him." She frowned. "I should have just grabbed him while I had the chance. I would have found out what he was after."

"You said he was armed. You weren't."

"Yes." She turned to look at Christine head-on. "So?"

Christine chuckled. "I wasn't impugning your competency, Alex. Merely pointing out that in those circumstances, with an opponent you haven't been able to assess, it's wisest to leave hand-to-hand combat as a last resort."

"Well," Alex groused, "at least we'd know who he was, or who sent him."

"We will," Christine said. "Eventually."

"I want to know now."

"Remember that old Dutch proverb, Alexandra."

"Yeah, yeah, I know. A handful of patience is worth more than a bushel of brains. But somebody else said you had to have patience to learn patience."

Christine chuckled. "It was always your biggest challenge, wasn't it?"

"Isn't it," Alex corrected her wryly, acknowledging the lifelong battle it would probably be for her.

"That you know it is still your challenge indicates you're winning the fight," Christine said, ever the wise mentor. "Of course, wandering around Athena at night isn't exactly new to you, now is it? After all, you're one of the few to actually see the Dark Angel."

Alex's eyes widened and she sucked in a breath. Christine smiled at her.

"Did you really think I didn't know what you girls called him?"

"I…we…"

Alex fumbled to a halt, a little amazed at how embarrassing it was now, looking back over the years at that bit of adolescent romanticizing.

"You were teenage girls," Christine said soothingly. "It's in the nature of the creature to romanticize something like that."

Alex's mouth quirked. "I suppose. And it did seem wildly romantic to us back then, this tall, dark and handsome guy so desperate to find out what happened to his sister that he broke in here."

"He was that. For him to come back after the first time we caught him here, when he was just a boy, he had to be desperate."

"It was crazy that he thought Athena had something to do with her death. I don't get that, his sister wasn't even a student here. But it was still romantic. That we never knew his name, or who he really was, just made it more so." Alex's smile faded. "I hadn't thought about him in years."

"Considering the celebrity seeing him made you, I'm surprised you could ever forget."

Alex's smile returned then, but it was touched with a lingering sadness. "He did increase my cachet considerably. I wonder whatever happened to him?"

Christine shrugged. "I don't know. I'm just glad we made the right decision in not prosecuting him for burglary. He never came back."

"It was just the desperation," Alex said with a shrug. "People do crazy things when someone they love…"

Her voice trailed off as she realized they were now in the same boat that young man had been in, over fifteen years ago. Were they crazy for believing there was more to Rainy's death than what the

officials believed? She didn't think so. So, were
they any different than he had been?

"I guess I understand him better now," she said,
her voice softened by emotional pain.

Christine smiled, a smile that was as pained as
Alex's voice had been. But her words were gentle,
approving. "You've come a long way, Alex. All the
Cassandras have. I'm so very proud of you all."

Alex saw the smile, saw the moisture in Christine's eyes, and guessed she also had been thinking about the new presence of death here in this
place they both loved.

"We'll find the truth about Rainy. I promise we
will," she said.

"I know you will."

A yawn crept up on Alex, and she couldn't quite
stop it. "I am tired," she admitted before Christine
could point out the undeniable fact.

"I should think you would be. I thought when
you finally hit the pillow last night that you'd be
out like a light for hours."

"So did I. I haven't really slept for more than a
couple of hours for—" she had to stop to calculate,
proving the truth of what she was saying "—almost forty-eight hours now."

"You'd better now. Stay here this time. I'll be
making some calls to step up security around here."

"I can't. I need to call Kayla, and then get over
to the morgue and take another look."

She was very aware of how unspecific she was
being, how vague, as if avoiding stating the fact

that it was the body of their friend she was talking about would somehow make it not true. And she knew by Christine's expression that she was just as aware. But she said nothing about it, merely nodded.

"You can call Kayla after you rest. You can't do anyone any good if you're so tired you can't think straight."

Alex opened her mouth to argue, to protest she could keep going. Saw the glint in Christine's good eye and capitulated so quickly it was almost embarrassing. Some old habits were very hard to break.

"Yes, ma'am," she said, with a meekness that would have astonished anyone who knew Alex but had never met Christine Evans. Christine occupied a unique place in the hearts and minds of all Athenans. She was both disciplinarian and inspiration, stern and gentle, and a teacher who was willing to learn from her students, all rolled into one. It was a rite of passage to earn the privilege of calling her Christine instead of Ms. Evans.

Alex did go to bed and knew she was beyond exhausted when the fold-out sofa bed felt like the most comfortable thing she'd ever slept on. This time she did sleep, and surprisingly the nightmares she had feared didn't come. She dreamed, but the tangled images of Rainy alive and smiling, telling them it was all a silly mistake, were somehow comforting. After a while even those stopped, and she slept deeply and barely remembered them when she woke up a few hours later.

The minute she sat up she knew Christine had been right. She felt much better. And ready to go. Ready to get to some answers.

And if need be, ready to fight.

There had to be something there, Alex thought as she paced the small morgue, waiting for the doctor to finish.

She had a feeling Christine had pulled some strings and called the woman in from neighboring Luke Air Force Base. Although Dr. Ellen Battaglia wasn't in uniform, she gave the impression. Alex recognized it because fellow Cassandra and air force captain Josie Lockworth had it, as well.

No one who met Josie was ever surprised to find out that she was a take charge woman, making a success of her air force career. And if that new stealth system she was working on for the Predator spy plane functioned as well as it was supposed to—something Alex didn't at all doubt, knowing Josie—there was likely no limit to how far she could go.

"Ready," the doctor said.

Taking a deep breath, Alex braced herself to look at a very intimate part of one of the dearest people in her life, excised from her body with cold steel. Then she turned around.

The doctor had set a gleaming silver metal tray on a table. Knowing what was in it, Alex had to once more beat down her emotions.

It's a scientific puzzle, just like anything else

you work on every day, she told herself. You can do this. You *have* to do this.

Still, the two small organs on the gleaming tray made her shiver. With a final effort, she made herself focus on the puzzle, of which these were just a single part. But perhaps a crucial part.

Now that she again saw what she'd seen previously, with plenty of time to look carefully, she was certain her first thought was right. And now she noticed something else, something that bothered her even more.

"Dr. Battaglia?"

The doctor, who had turned away with a welcome sensitivity, turned back. "Yes?"

Alex pointed to the areas on the outer surface of the ovaries. "If you had to guess…how old would you say those scars are?"

The woman leaned over for a closer examination. "These things can be tricky," she said. "There are so many variables. I'd guess they are older, but I'd hate to testify to an exact age. I'll take some tissue samples, that may help. But one thing I can say with some certainty."

"What?"

"The majority of those scars are the same age."

"The same age?" Alex's breath caught. If all those scars were made at the same time, then her suspicions had to be correct. "And the regularity of the spacing," she said. "It looks…mechanical."

The doctor nodded. "I noticed that, as well. No, those scars aren't the result of natural monthly ovulation. But the work is somewhat sloppy. As if someone was in a hurry."

Or scared?

"Work, you said. Something was done to her," Alex whispered, fighting down a growing feeling of dread.

"I'd say so. A procedure of some kind. Was she undergoing fertility treatments?"

"Yes, but only recently."

The doctor frowned. "That doesn't fit. That's what the scars look like, sloppy or hurried harvesting, but these aren't recent."

Alex fought off the ripples of nausea that the scenes in her imagination were causing. "Could what was done to her be done and leave a scar that would look like a routine appendectomy?"

"Absolutely. In this case a bikini scar, such as…your friend has."

A bikini scar.

A new thought careened into her mind, and Alex had to suppress a shiver as Dr. Battaglia turned and went to work getting her tissue samples.

A bikini scar. A fake appendectomy. Mechanical puncturelike marks on the ovaries.

What had happened to Rainy?

Alex left the morgue quickly. This time, as she stepped outside, she welcomed the blast of heat that hit her. She blinked against the brilliant desert sun and freed a tangled strand of curly hair from the strap of her shoulder bag-cum-holster. She pulled her sunglasses out and slid them on.

She walked to her car, careful not to touch any metal part while unlocking it. Got in. Set her bag on the passenger seat. Slid the key into the ignition. Started the motor. Flipped on the air.

She concentrated on each routine step as if it could not be done with anything less than full attention.

She leaned back in the driver's seat. After a few moments the blast of air from the rental's vents began to come out cooler, soothing her flushed skin but doing nothing at all for her tangled, wild emotions.

And finally, finally, she let the thought she'd been fighting surface.

She had her own bikini scar. From when she'd had her own appendix out, junior year.

Or she thought she had.

More memories flooded her. Rainy soothing her, saying this made them more sisters than ever, and joking about Athena's water supply causing appendicitis.

But Rainy had never had her appendix out. Instead, she'd had some ominous procedure done, something to do with her ovaries, likely her eggs.

Alex knew she was making a lot of assumptions on circumstantial evidence, but her gut was telling her she was right. That those scars were as old as Rainy's supposed appendectomy. It only made sense. Perhaps whatever had made them had rendered her infertile, hence her inability to conceive when she and Marshall had so desperately wanted a child.

What if her own operation was also a hoax? What if it had been a fake of some kind, the abdominal pain induced artificially? Perhaps exacerbated by drugs she thought had been given to help?

What if what had been done to Rainy had been done to her?

Alex sat there for a long time. The very idea of such a deeply personal, intimate violation made her stomach churn, and brought sweat to her skin despite the now chilly blast of the air-conditioning.

She had never thought much about having children, and when she did, it was off in the future somewhere while she concentrated on her career in the here and now. Although she had empathized with Rainy's quest, she had often doubted that she would be horrifically upset if she herself never had children at all.

But that was before she came face-to-face with the outrageous possibility that that choice had been stolen from her, taken away without her knowledge or consent.

This scraped raw something in the very core of her being. Her world, her whole life, while never dull, had always been within her control. Academics and athletics came easily to her, and she chose what courses she would take and then proceeded to excel in them. Then she had decided to show her parents and her grandfather that she wouldn't always dance to their tune, and had done so.

In the face of her grandfather's disappointment she had then decided she'd made her point and worked hard to turn it around. And she had learned quickly that the rigid expectations she'd feared at Athena were in fact the keys to doors too often locked against women in the world.

Athena's stated goal was to open those doors, expand possibilities and promote opportunities in all fields for women. The bigger picture included empowering women far beyond just the workplace. But above all, the goal was to help students find the person they were meant to be. They were never pushed or prodded in any direction, only given the tools necessary to make the right choice, and the chance to make that choice work.

Choice.

Such a simple thing. *Or it should be.*

She thought again of Rainy's craving for a baby. Of the nights she'd spent on the phone listening to her old friend talk about it, so longingly.

"You never had a chance, Rainy," Alex murmured. "And maybe now, neither do I."

A slow, burgeoning heat began to build in her. She recognized it for what it was, a rising anger. It would reach the level of red-hot fury, she was sure, before this was over. But then it would cool, set and become rational, become the driving force of a woman with the knowledge and tools to exact retribution.

"Hurt one Cassandra, hurt us all," she spoke into the now chilly air of the car. "Use one of us, and all of us will exact payment. Whoever you are, whatever your goal, you will regret it."

The moment she cleared the dead zone, that brief stretch along Olympus Road where her cell service always failed, her phone beeped at her. She quickly dialed her voice mail to play her messages. There were two, the first from Christine letting her know she was still off campus, finishing up interviews with a couple of potential instructors.

A smiled quirked one corner of Alex's mouth. She didn't envy the applicants, who were likely expecting a typical job interview. An interview for Athena Academy was anything but typical. No one was even brought to the school until they had passed both the initial and secondary screenings, and the first interview with Christine. And they only got that far if they passed an extensive background check.

The second message was from Kayla. It was short. A bit cryptic. And very disturbing.

She had searched Rainy's papers and her computer at home and at her office, and was now reluctantly working with a police detective who was looking into Rainy's accident. Reluctantly, because Kayla was as protective of Athena Academy as Alex and all Athena graduates were. And the suspicion Kayla had developed about Rainy's death echoed Alex's deepest fear.

Someone at Athena was part of it.

Chapter 5

Odd, Alex thought. She believed Kayla, trusted her suspicions. Or perhaps not odd; after all, it had never been Kayla's intelligence or abilities that had been in question, only her judgment.

The judgment of a teenage girl, Alex reminded herself. And only her judgment about men.

That teenage Kayla, in hot-blooded anger and at the height of their dispute over just that, had said Alex could never understand how she felt about Mike because Alex would never climb down off her high horse long enough to let a man get close to her.

Alex had been stung, painfully, that of all people her closest friend would throw that accusation at her. Strangers had often assumed she was a snob before they'd even met her, simply because she was a Forsythe and had the Forsythe millions behind her. She'd developed a reserve because of it, which had in turn fed the image. But she'd never thought to hear it from a friend. Let alone her best friend.

Besides, she'd proven Kayla wrong. She and Emerson would be married...sometime. He'd been pressing her for a date, but she'd continued to put him off. Something always seemed to get in the way—her work, his work, something. She had a heavy caseload this month, he had a big operation scheduled, or a trip for a consultation the next month. Something always interfered. Their mothers had both threatened to intervene and take over, but fortunately so far she and Emerson had managed to stave that off.

But she had never expected anything like this to be the roadblock. She couldn't even begin to think about a wedding with Rainy gone like this, and her death shrouded in inconsistencies and suspicions. And if that gave Alex a vague sense of relief, she didn't dwell on it now.

Kayla had been wrong, of course.

And then, for the first time in years, the rest of what her fellow Cassandra had said came back to her.

Unless you happen to find a guy who's on as high a horse as you are, Kayla had added, just before she'd slammed the phone down on the last conversation they would have for a very long time.

Alex's mouth tightened. Emerson certainly rode a high horse, and she had no doubt he was exactly the kind of guy Kayla had been referring to. His family was one of the oldest and wealthiest in Virginia, almost in the Forsythe stratosphere, as Kayla had called it.

She had been teasing then. At least, Alex always thought she had been. But in the end the bitterness all came out, as if it had been too long bottled up, and a friendship that was as close as sisterhood had been shattered. Alex had always hoped they might someday heal the breach, but neither of them had ever made the move.

And now they had to deal with each other. In a sad way, Rainy had brought them together again, as she had all those years ago.

Christine was still out when Alex returned to her bungalow. Alex paced, trying to decide whether to call her and risk interrupting an interview.

"She's probably got her phone off," Alex told herself aloud as she crossed the small but comfortable living room. Christine had lived here since the beginning of Athena, and she'd made a warm, welcoming home out of what could easily have been cold, impersonal staff housing.

Not for the first time Alex wondered at how thoroughly Christine, an attractive, vibrant woman, had given herself to Athena. She seemed to have no life outside the school, and dedicated herself to the students completely. Alex had often wondered if she herself would ever feel so passionately about anything.

Now she knew. Because the need to find the truth about Rainy's death was consuming her. And that was a bottom line she knew Christine would understand. She made the call, just in case the principal was finished and on her way back, but as she'd expected got her voice mail. She spelled out the situation quickly, as much as she felt safe doing over a cell-phone call, and told Christine what she planned to do. She knew Christine would okay her next step.

Unfortunately, Christine had the master keys with her. She kept them on hand at all times, just in case.

"I'm going to be a B and E master before this is over," she muttered. This was putting her lock-picking and breaking-and-entering skills to the test. It was a good thing she'd brought her picks along with her other gear.

But since there was no other way in, and she knew she'd never be able to wait until Christine returned with her master keys, she checked to make sure she had the necessary tools and headed out for the science building, which held the small medical facility. While lock picking wasn't one of the skills she'd honed at the bureau, her lessons at Athena weren't that long ago.

At least here if she was caught, the worst she'd face would be explaining to Betsy Stone, Athena Academy's nurse, what she was doing. The woman could be a bit territorial about her domain. But Betsy hadn't yet returned from the term break, although according to Christine she was due in later today. Alex would be able to talk to her then about Rainy's "appendectomy."

I wonder if Betsy is still as determinedly blond as ever, she thought as she walked around to the rear doors that opened into the hallway just outside the entrance to the small infirmary.

Nearing fifty now, the nurse had been at Athena since the beginning, like Christine. She, however, was much harder to get to know. Alex knew Christine's former army commander, Lieutenant General Snyder, had sent Betsy to Athena, and it seemed to have worked well for all concerned. Betsy didn't inspire the kind of loyalty that Christine did, but her frank manner and easy competence earned her respect.

Alex sorted out a pick to use on the building, wondering when they would finally make the upgrade to a card key system, with fingerprint ID or some other more advanced method. Not that there was any need for it here.

At least, there hadn't been, she thought as she reached for the knob.

The door was already unlocked. And partially open.

Alex stared at the door that stood ajar by a fraction of an inch. Despite being followed last night, she felt safe here on Athena grounds, and it took a moment for her instincts to kick in. It could be just an oversight, but she couldn't make herself believe it, not now.

Again she'd come unarmed, never expecting to need a weapon here, at what felt more like home to her than anyplace else. But if someone was here, she could lose them if she went back to retrieve her sidearm now.

From now on I bring the thing if I have to carry it in my teeth, she vowed as she inched the door open. It made no sound; everything at Athena was in good repair.

When she discovered that the inside door to the infirmary was also open, she knew this was more than mere oversight.

She spotted him in the corner, near the bank of file cabinets that had been her own goal. He had a drawer open, his dark head bent over it as he flipped through the hanging file folders inside. Adrenaline surged. She was certain she was about to add another sizable piece of the solution to the puzzle of Rainy's death.

But first she had to make sure he didn't get away. She used every muscle in her body to make her approach stealthy, all the while preparing to attack if necessary. She knew she hadn't made a noise, but when she was still a good ten feet away he seemed to sense her presence. His head came up, and he started to turn.

Alex leaped over the desk in between them and let her momentum carry her forward, using her full weight not to tackle the man, who was clearly bigger than she was, but to slam against the drawer he'd been going through. She heard him swear as the drawer smashed shut on his arm, effectively pinning him.

She relaxed too soon. The man made a sweeping move with one leg and took her legs out from under her. It was enough for him to free his arm and he moved around the desk toward the door. She instinctively rolled to her feet, already planning her next move. She was reaching for a heavy-looking bottle on the counter when he yelled.

"Hold it!"

She saw no reason to obey, no matter the commanding presence in his voice or the fact that he hadn't run out the door. He was the trespasser here, not her. She grabbed the bottle.

"I'm FBI, damn it, stand down!"

Well, that explained the commanding presence. She didn't release the bottle, but she straightened up to look at him.

"You're what?"

"A federal agent."

He held a hand up, palm out to indicate he wasn't going for a gun, then reached into his jacket with two fingers. She had only seconds to decide whether to believe his innocent intentions. But his hand stopped short of where a shoulder holster would be, and he pulled out the standard issue black ID case, badge on one side, ID card on the other.

She was too far away to read the name, but it looked just like hers. Except for the stern, square-

jawed picture, of course. It might be real. He had
the air.

Her mouth quirked downward at one corner as
she looked at him more carefully.

Well, now, aren't you just a recruiter's dream?
Poster boy for the finest Feebie tradition. Tall, dark
and handsome, the whole bit.

The only bit of comfort she could find in the tab-
leau was the crease between his brows as he rubbed
at the arm she'd smashed in the file cabinet.

Score one for the girls.

He seemed vaguely familiar, in a way that tick-
led the edge of her mind without crystallizing.
Could she have seen him at FBI headquarters? Not
likely if he was assigned in Arizona. And she
couldn't have forgotten those blue-green eyes. It
was a question she wanted an answer to, but not
before the main one, which she asked now.

"What are you doing here?"

"Investigating," he said with a shrug she found
very annoying.

"Oh, really," she said, eyeing him levelly, keeping her cool though her pulse went up another
notch. FBI, investigating Athena? And she didn't
know? "Investigating what?"

"It's classified."

She relaxed a little. He was bluffing. "On private property? Without permission or a warrant?"

"No one was here to ask."

"And I'm sure that will fly with the SIC," she said.

He frowned slightly, whether it was at her use

of the FBI terminology for special agent in charge, her lack of awe at his federal presence or perhaps just the pain in his arm she didn't know. Maybe it was all of those.

And then he stiffened.

"What the hell is going on in here?" The voice from the doorway made her jump. "What are you doing in my clinic?"

Betsy Stone stood there, looking shocked. The shock was replaced by a frown of recognition as she looked at Alex.

Alex glanced at the man and was startled by the cold expression on his face. He didn't turn around to face Betsy Stone. He watched as Betsy walked toward Alex, his expression even colder.

"Wait, I know you. You're the Forsythe girl, aren't you? Alexandra?"

Alex suppressed a grimace. To some people she supposed that's what she would always be, the Forsythe girl. With her illustrious last name her only real value.

"I found him here," she said, implying that that was the reason for her own presence. No sense in confessing to her own plans if she didn't have to. Let this intruder take the heat for everything. Betsy Stone blocked her view for a moment and Alex shifted to keep him in sight.

"And I'll leave Ms. Forsythe to explain, I'm late for an appointment."

Alex had realized what he was doing even as he turned and slipped out the door. She leaped back over the desk but had to avoid the startled Betsy and lost precious seconds moving her bodily out of the way. By the time she reached the door, he was nowhere in sight.

As she'd suspected, Betsy Stone had been reluctant to have Alex go through the files without Christine's okay. Alex had had to control her temper and wait for Christine to return from her interview, knowing she'd run out of time.

Now she tapped on Christine's door and called out to announce her presence. When Christine called back for her to come in, she pulled the door open and stepped inside, savoring for a brief moment the rush of cool, air-conditioned air. Christine stepped out of the bedroom, where she'd apparently just changed into casual pants and a sleeveless blouse. She looked fit, trim and much younger than her sixty-one years.

"How was the interview?"

"Oh, it went well enough. I liked him, but he's really not cut out for Athena. Very learned, very intelligent, but too ponderous. It takes a quick wit to keep up with the caliber of students we have here. The girls would cut him to ribbons his first day in class."

Alex smiled, hating to break Christine's good mood. "You missed more excitement here. I found a man claiming to be FBI going through files in the infirmary."

Christine went still. "An FBI agent was here? At Athena?"

"So he said. I take it you haven't heard about any kind of investigation."

"No. I would have told you."

Alex hadn't realized she'd been a little tense until she relaxed at Christine's answer.

"I'd like permission for Kayla or I to have access to medical files. In case there's a clue somewhere about Rainy."

Christine frowned and walked across the room to pick up the phone. She spoke for a few minutes, then came back.

"Betsy has my instructions to give you access. I assume it will be Kayla, since you're leaving early in the morning."

Alex nodded. "I'll be back for the funeral."

Before packing, Alex called Kayla to ask her to follow up on the files and to tell her about the man in the infirmary. After they hung up, Alex's thoughts whirled.

Had the man been sent by the FBI to investigate Athena? Or was he somehow involved in Rainy's death?

One thing was certain. If the handsome stranger was really FBI, Alex would soon know it. Because although he'd gotten away, he'd left his fingerprints behind.

Chapter 6

The last thing Alex wanted to do was leave Athena Academy with nothing resolved, but she had no choice. Her gut was screaming she was going in the wrong direction from the time she left Athena all the way to the airport. But she had to get back to work to finish up some cases, and she had to do it now so she could be free to get back to Arizona for Rainy's yet to be scheduled funeral.

She suppressed a shudder at the thought as she fastened her seat belt and settled in for the long flight back to D.C. She was grateful she didn't have to make arrangements, and her heart ached for Marshall, who did. She hoped Kayla would help him. Not that it would be any easier for her.

She pushed the button on the armrest to lean her seat back.

She began to think about the work awaiting her. On the letter-bomb case, they needed a mitochondrial DNA analysis to either confirm or eliminate a newly arrested suspect. She needed to finish the report on those carpet fibers she'd matched to a suspect's vehicle and start the analysis on the wood splinters that had been pulled from the wounds of the murder victim from New Jersey.

She smothered a yawn and closed her eyes, not expecting to drift off.

To her surprise, she slept, and only the building pressure in her ears as they began the descent to Dulles Airport woke her.

She'd gotten lucky and been able to park in the newer daily garage, where it was only a walk of a couple hundred yards to the terminal and she could avoid the shuttle and the moving sidewalks so many tourists couldn't seem to figure out how to use.

She was vaguely aware, as always, of the distinctive architecture of the airport terminal, the slanting, curved glass walls that let in so much light and looked so unique from the outside, especially capped by the off-center, concave roof. But she was only vaguely aware of it; she was back in big-city mode that quickly.

She reached her car in minutes, mentally preparing herself every step of the way for negotiating the traffic.

When it came time to choose between making

the turn to Alexandria to the forty-year-old colonial built by her grandfather that she called home, or to her grandfather's horse farm in Middleburg, she hesitated. Her plan had been to go straight home, call Emerson, grab some more sleep and head to the office in the morning.

But she could feel now that she'd had enough sleep on the plane to keep going. And enough that going right to sleep again would be difficult.

She had to decide now; east to I-495, or down to US-50 and west. There was only ten miles difference in the distance, but the drives were vastly different, one through the crowded streets of the D.C. metro area to Alexandria, the other to the horse country of northern Virginia. The destinations were different, as well, worlds apart in pace, philosophy and mood.

She turned her back on the city.

She told herself she wanted to see Lacy again, but deep down she knew what she was doing. She was running for home. She was hurting inside, and she was running for the one place outside Athena where she'd always found comfort. The one person who had always provided it.

Even when his own heart had been broken at the death of his only son, Alex's father, in a plane crash, her grandfather had been there for her. He had been even more devastated than either she or her brother; their father had traveled for the family business most of their lives and she felt as if they'd barely known him.

Sometimes she had felt awkward in the face of her grandfather's grief, thinking she should be feeling at least as bad, but the hole in her life just hadn't been as big. It had brought both her and her brother closer to their grandfather, and it had been some time before she had realized that was likely for his sake as much as theirs.

Charles Forsythe, unlike many of his generation, had embraced the electronic age with delight, realizing early on that it would enable him to work—which in his case meant overseeing the Forsythe fortune—from his beloved farm. He still maintained an office in Washington, owned a flat in London, had held on to the house Alex was now living in—making her Alexandra from Alexandria, as her too-witty brother had often pointed out—and had a condo on the West Coast. But the farm was his true home.

Her grandmother, who also had died when Alex was a child, had been strictly citified and was the only reason her grandfather had built the elegant, well-situated Alexandria house. But her grandfather had been a country boy at heart, and that heart was here in Virginia horse country.

She thought of calling ahead to make sure he was still up, but decided against it. He was a night owl and rarely went to bed before midnight, so nine would be nothing. Besides, she enjoyed the idea of surprising him.

She set the cruise control on her Lexus SUV for the long, straight stretch of Route 50, glad to be back in her own car. And glad that she'd chosen to do this. It wouldn't be much longer to get to the city tomorrow from the farm than it would be from Alexandria, and she'd relax more here. She had never, she admitted reluctantly now, felt completely at home in the big house on the edge of the Belle Haven country club on the west bank of the Potomac. It was lovely, the setting beautiful, but it had never felt like home.

Not her home, anyway. And it wasn't simply that her grandmother had had a taste for floral wallpaper and curtains that she didn't share. She'd decided recently that it must just be that she was so often only there to sleep. If she had a normal job, with normal hours, she would have spent more time there and it would have become a home to her, instead of just the place she happened to kick her shoes off.

She got off the main road, making the turns from there with the automatic ease that comes from long familiarity. With each turn her eagerness grew; this had definitely been the right decision.

Forsythe Farms was marked with a small, unadorned sign that could easily be missed. Its simplicity belied the fact that one of the nation's wealthiest men lived there. Long a billionaire, her grandfather believed in putting his money only in things he firmly believed in or had a passion for. Even the house in upscale Alexandria was worth under a million—although he could have afforded many times that—because he didn't believe in flaunting what he had. He lived quite comfortably, in the manner necessary for his position, but nowhere near what he could have afforded.

She made the turn onto the drive, pressing the series of numbers and then the release button on her specially-designed personal remote to open the power gate that crossed the drive a few yards in from the road.

There were only two other openers for this gate in existence, her grandfather's and her brother's. Any other attempt to open the gate would set off an alarm. Each opener had a different code, to make breaking in more difficult should one be lost or stolen.

There was also a small button on the back side that would deactivate the device and send an alarm. In that way it could also be used as a duress sign if necessary. It was hardly standard FBI issue, but for a Forsythe, it was the kind of security you grew up with. Kidnapping was a possibility all the Forsythes lived with from the day they were born.

The gate also triggered a signal at the house. Her grandfather would know now she was coming—assuming he wasn't expecting Ben, as well—but the surprise would still be fresh enough when she got to the house.

She drove through the gate, watching in her rearview mirror to be sure no one tried to get through behind her. When it was secure, she continued up the winding drive. She knew the drive well, drove it easily even in the dark. She could

picture the gently rolling landscape, dotted with
hickory, ash and maple trees, divided by rail fences. If it was daylight, she'd be able to see the
yearlings on the right, the mares and the latest crop
of foals on the left. She missed the frolicking of
the gangly-legged babies in the rich grass more
than anything.

She pulled up near the garage of the sprawling,
ranch-style house. She could see a light on in her
grandfather's study, the big, book-lined room with
the bay window that looked out over the paddocks
and the main barn.

He answered the door himself, and she guessed
he'd sent the staff to bed already. Things started
early around here, and it was the sort of thing he
would think of even though he himself ran on
much less sleep than he expected of his employ-
ees. The casual thoughtfulness was the sort of
thing that made his people intensely loyal.

It was the sort of thing he'd hammered into his
grandchildren, as well. It had taken, completely,
with her. Ben was another story. He seemed determined to set new records for urbane uselessness.

"I'm delighted to see you, my dear," her grandfather said as he ushered her inside. "Surprised, but
delighted." He glanced at her small suitcase, noted
the tags still fastened to the handle. "You just flew
in?"

She nodded. He paused in the entry, taking a
look at her for the first time under the light of the
elegant but subtle foyer chandelier.

"You come with me," he ordered.

She followed meekly. One didn't argue with Charles Bennington Forsythe. So when he led her to his study, gestured her into a chair, went to the small bar in the far corner and poured an inch of rich amber liquid into a small snifter, she took it without resistance.

The unmistakable aroma of amaretto hit her nose and made her breathe deeply. Leave it to him to know exactly what she needed. She swirled it, breathed in some more, and then at last took a small sip. The sweetness coated her tongue, the heat warmed her all the way down, and at last she sank back in the rich green leather wingback chair and let her weary body relax.

For a long, silent moment her grandfather studied her. Then, his voice soft and gentle, he said, "There are no words to ease your pain, Alex, so I won't try. I will simply say I'm sorry, and that not just you but the world is the poorer for Lorraine's loss."

Tears stung her eyelids. Her grandfather always seemed to know the right words to say. And it was true, Rainy was a loss to more than just her friends and family. The things she would now never do, the children she would never raise to be as strong and smart and good as she had been....

She blinked rapidly, took another sip of the liqueur to fortify herself. She was tired, had just managed to relax, but she knew she had to gear up again. Realized now the real reason behind what had seemed at the time a casual decision to come here rather than go home to that big, empty house. While she had wanted the comforting presence of her grandfather, there was another reason to come here.

"G.C.?"

"Yes?"

She took a deep breath, then made the plunge. "Something was going on with Rainy. I'm not convinced the crash was an accident."

Charles, who had been lounging in his matching wing chair, straightened. He set down his own glass and turned his full attention on her, leaning forward.

"What have you found?"

Bless you, G.C.

Quickly, she gave him the rundown of the facts they'd discovered, wanting to hear his own impressions before she gave him their suspicions. She was open about some of the information coming from Kayla. Although he knew they hadn't spoken in a very long time, he said nothing, clearly recognizing the priority here just as they had.

When she was done, he leaned back, propping his elbows on the arms of the leather chair, steepling his elegant fingers in front of him. It was a habit she'd adopted as a child to try and be as like him as she could, a habit that long ago she'd learned meant he was thinking and was not to be disturbed. She sat back herself and took a last sip of the amaretto while she waited for whatever conclusion he would reach. She wondered if he remembered her own supposed appendectomy all those years ago, but said nothing. Her situation would simply have to wait.

"I'm not an investigator," he began.

Alex waved off the disclaimer. "You have the best mind I've ever known."

"Thank you, my dear girl. I knew there was a reason I adored you."

Despite her frame of mind, one corner of her mouth quirked upward. For her grandfather did adore her, and she knew it. She'd always known it. It went a long way toward making up for the aloofness of her mother and the absence of her long dead father.

"So. While there could be an innocent explanation for each one of these things, if your gut is telling you otherwise, listen to it."

Alex let out a long breath, not realizing until now how much she had needed to hear that. She didn't think it had been audible, but her grandfather smiled.

"You have the best mind *I've* ever known," he said.

A rush of emotion filled her. "G.C., what would I have done without you?" she asked, her voice tight.

"You would have managed. You've always been as tough as you had to be."

"I come from tough stock," she said. She imitated his most dignified and impressive tone of voice. "'Forsythes helped build this country.'"

"Well, we did," he said sternly, then ruined the

effect by chuckling at his own pomposity, as he always did. "And now you're helping keep it safe," he added.

"I do my bit. As much as one can do from a lab," she said, still fighting down strong emotions.

"Which is a great deal, these days. Many cases are won and lost on your turf. Speaking of which, how is that new lab working out?"

"Not bad, for a mere hundred and thirty mil," she said, already feeling more under control.

This was something she could talk about. The new FBI lab at the academy in Quantico was beyond cutting edge, and a quantum leap above their crowded old quarters in the downtown D.C. building, giving them half a million square feet, three times the space they'd had before.

"The first few months were a learning curve, but we're pretty well settled in now."

"At least you're in a lab that's designed to be a lab," he said.

"You mean instead of a converted set of offices? Yes. And with the labs separate from the offices and everything else, it's made integrity of evidence and chain-of-custody much easier to maintain. Not to mention having separate setups for microscopy, wet chemistry, biological sciences and all the rest."

"It's farther for you."

"But a nicer drive." She eyed him for a moment. "Thank you for the distraction. I'm okay now."

Charles Forsythe didn't deny or dissemble, and

she appreciated that. "I'm glad I was here to do it. I'm off to Tokyo next week, you know."

"I'd forgotten. I'm very glad you're still here."

He looked at her intently. "What are you going to do?"

She knew he was no longer talking about the new FBI lab, or her commute.

"Keep going," she said. "We owe it to Rainy."

"Is there anything I can do to help?"

Alex opened her mouth to say no, then stopped. And thought. Her grandfather was, after all, on the Athena board of directors. True, he was an absentee member, but still privy to the inner workings.

Not to mention that he'd been involved in the development of the school from the beginning, when it was merely an idea. He'd been involved with planning Athena before Rainy had begun school there and had had her now possibly fictional attack of appendicitis.

"Do you remember anything unusual, anything from way back, happening at Athena?"

"Like what?"

That she couldn't help with. "I'm not sure." She shrugged, hating the vagueness of what she was feeling. "Anything that would give anybody a grudge against Athena, or someone from Athena?"

"You mean beyond the usual resentment of a frightened sexist, male or female?"

"Yes. Anyone who might want to do more than just stew about whatever his beef is."

Again he steepled his hands in front of him. Silence reigned. He thought for a very long time before slowly shaking his head.

"Athena's been remarkably clear of that kind of thing, in part I think because we've kept such a low profile. Most of those who know of it are supportive. Oh, there are some out there who know and don't like it, and a few who feel threatened by the idea and would like to see it shut down."

This was not news to Alex. She knew that many of the very places Athena was training women to become part of were run by those who felt threatened by the idea of capable, trained, strong women moving in. Those people would just as soon see the proverbial glass ceiling changed to one of reinforced concrete.

"But I don't know of anyone who'd overtly try to derail it," her grandfather went on. "At least, not in such a public way as murder."

Alex sighed. She didn't miss the implication that Athena's enemies were more covert. She'd expected that, too.

"What about that student, the only one ever to be expelled from Athena?" he asked.

"Shannon Conner? I thought about her right away, but I don't think she'd bother. If she's after anyone, it's Tory, not Rainy."

"Is she smart enough?"

Alex thought about the nasty, jealous blonde who had tried to frame Josie Lockworth for theft but had been exposed by Tory's determined investigation. Easily the most famous Cassandra, Victoria Patton was now a New York based television news reporter. And Shannon Conner had hated her from the day Tory had uncovered the truth that had humiliated Shannon and resulted in her expulsion. In fact, Shannon was now a reporter herself, on a rival network, as if even today the competition continued.

"Yes," Alex said finally. "And shrewd enough."

"Vindictive?"

"I haven't seen her in years, so I can't say. Back then…maybe. I'll dig into her a bit more," she said. "Do you remember any employee who left under duress, or resented being let go?"

"I suppose there must have been some in all these years, but I'd be willing to bet not many. Christine does too good a job screening…."

His voice trailed off and Alex saw his eyes take on that thoughtful gleam she knew so well.

"G.C.?"

"I was just remembering, there was a professor, a…Dr. Bradley, I think. No, Bradford. That was it. He taught for a year or so at Athena. But something happened there, between him and Christine."

"A disagreement?"

"I don't know exactly, but she called to ask the board to confirm she had total authority over personnel, and to advise them that she would not be asking him to return. This was the year after Athena opened, and we were still feeling our way."

"I'll look into that, too."

Alex pondered whether to mention Kayla's suspicion that someone inside Athena was involved with what had happened to Rainy. At last she decided not to, at least not yet. She wasn't afraid of what her grandfather might do; he believed too strongly in Athena and its goal to withdraw support now, just when the graduates were beginning to make their mark all around the world. But she decided to wait until she talked more with Kayla and found out exactly what had roused her suspicions in that area.

She bade her grandfather good-night with a hug and a kiss and retreated to the room that had been hers since childhood. It still held some souvenirs of that time, her huge collection of Breyer horses, her show ribbons and pictures of Lacy from her birth to this spring.

The big bed had at one time held the frilly, sheer canopy her grandmother had picked out for her. As a teen she had switched to the more exotic and much more to her taste mosquito netting that hung there now. Once it had enabled her to pretend she was on safari.

A photo safari, of course; she was no hunter. At least, not of innocent animals. Their less-innocent, supposed superiors were another matter altogether. There was at least one out there now that she would hunt to the ground.

Chapter 7

Alex awoke wondering if there was any smell as potent or as alluring as freshly brewed coffee in the morning. Sleepily she sat up, straightened the huge T-shirt she'd slept in, ran a hand through her tousled hair and pulled on a pair of socks in lieu of the slippers she never seemed to remember to pack, mainly because she didn't like wearing them. And for that reason she didn't bother to look in the closet, where there was likely a pair or two of the ones her mother insisted on buying her lingering.

Still yawning, she shuffled down the long hallway and across the living room with its rich mahogany floor, thinking she'd be better off if she headed out for a dip in the pool. But the coffee was still beckoning, and like a mouse working its way through the maze to the cheese she made her way to the kitchen, already imagining the quick jolt of hot caffeine. Thank goodness that was a vice her grandfather refused to give up.

She pushed open the swinging door, wondering if it was G.C. who had started the brew, or Sylvia Barrett, the cook and housekeeper of nearly twenty years.

It was neither. The man at the counter heard the door open behind him and turned. Smiled.

"Hi, sis. I heard you were here."

Bennington Forsythe was tall, handsome and utterly charming. She supposed all that was a requirement for what appeared to be his chosen role in life, that of rich, devil-may-care playboy. It was a role that clearly pleased him and greatly irritated her—she hated seeing his tremendous potential wasted—and was tolerated with a surprising forbearance by their grandfather.

She'd wondered for a long time now why Ben had turned out the way he had. It made no sense to her. He had never shown any sign growing up that he would end up this way. She wondered, not for the first time, if something had happened to him, something she didn't know about, that had changed the course of his life so dramatically, from most likely to succeed to most likely to blow it all.

"So how's my favorite FBI agent?"

"Surprised. I didn't expect to see you."

She knew her brother loved her, it glowed in his

eyes, but she doubted there was another woman on the planet who could say that with certainty. Not even their mother, whom they both tolerated more out of duty than genuine love. That the feeling was mutual was something they had both understood from an early age.

In moments when she succumbed to the pop-psychology kind of snap analysis, she wondered if Ben was chasing all those women trying to find the love he'd never gotten from their mother. And more than once she'd thought that what he needed was the perfect Athena to take him in hand. One that met her rather stringent standards for a sister-in-law, of course. She'd love to sic her on Ben and watch the fireworks. She had no doubt who would win, and it would probably be the best thing that could ever happen to him. But so far she'd managed to restrain herself.

"You're giving me that look again." Ben's tone was teasing, but the look in his eyes was suddenly weary. She expected the teasing, it was their standard sibling communication method, but weary was a new note.

"Which look is that, brother mine?"

"The one you always give me right before you launch into your patented 'When are you going to stop wasting your life?' lecture."

"Well, when are you?"

"I'll have you know there are women around the world who wish I had more to waste." The weariness was gone now. Or hidden behind the insouciant manner he sooner or later always seemed to resort to.

"I'm sure. So, where did you blow in from this time? Monaco? Rio?"

"Rome, actually."

"Ah. The Sophia Loren look-alike."

"One can only hope she ages as well," Ben said airily.

Alex busied herself pouring a mug of coffee, wishing she could learn not to care about her big brother's peccadilloes. But in her heart he was still the thirteen-year-old who had taught his ten-year-old sister how to fight and win against the bigger, stronger class bully who had tried to make her life hell simply because she was a Forsythe.

In fact, if she thought about it, Ben probably had almost as much to do with her success at Athena as their grandfather had. Charles Forsythe had opened her mind to the myriad possibilities, but Bennington Forsythe had taught her the tough stuff, how to use her brain and her own kind of strength to take on just about anyone or anything, no matter if it was bigger or stronger. He'd even taught her which feminine wiles usually worked best on what man. Things, he'd told her, that he wished his women didn't know, but that he was glad his little sister did.

She picked up her coffee and turned around to face him, leaning back against the smooth, cool granite counter and looking at him over the rim of the mug.

"And what's that look for? Or should I merely enjoy and not ask?"

She smiled at her brother. "Just thinking that if it wasn't for you, I wouldn't be where I am today."

Ben drew back slightly. "What?"

"You taught me an awful lot, big bro. And if I never thanked you for it, I'm thanking you now." She took a sip and enjoyed his slightly bewildered look.

"You women," he said at last, "are the strangest bunch of critters I've ever met."

She was saved from answering that bemused observation by the appearance of their grandfather, who looked inordinately pleased to have both of his grandchildren under his roof again. They had a leisurely breakfast, Alex deciding it was rare enough that the three of them were together that it warranted her taking the time.

Her brother and grandfather spent some time discussing the stock market and the world market, and as Alex listened—anyone with a chance to eavesdrop on Charles Forsythe's financial wisdom who didn't take advantage was a fool—she wondered how much of Ben's trust fund was left now, two years after he'd come into it at thirty. Although she'd grown up with money, the idea of inheriting millions of dollars on her next birthday simply boggled the mind.

It didn't seem to have ever affected Ben. He was happily spending away on his riotous lifestyle apparently without a second thought. Still, she couldn't help adoring him, and hid her qualms as best she could, knowing by now that there was little to nothing she could do about how he chose to live his life. It would take a more powerful force than his little sister to make him change.

I'll do something better with mine, she promised silently, not for the first time. She wasn't sure what yet, but she'd put it to some good use.

And none of it, not Ben's, not hers, not even her grandfather's billions, could give her the one thing she wanted most—Rainy, alive and well and laughing at the things Alex chose to worry about.

All the old emotions began to well up inside her, threatening to drown her in more useless tears. She got to her feet abruptly.

"I'm going for a ride before I have to head back to the city," she said.

Ben looked surprised, but G.C. didn't. "Twill could use some work," was all he said.

Alex nodded and went back to her room to change into the riding pants and boots she always left here for these occasions. She started to walk down the hill to the stable, a long, pristine white building with a green roof in a clearing full of rich grass, a matching green to the roof even at this time of year. But after a few strides she was trotting, then running, suffused with the feeling that only a hammering run over her grandfather's near one thousand acres would release the pressure building inside her.

Jacob Garner, the head groom who had worked for her grandfather for over thirty years, lit up when he saw her.

"Alex! It's been too long, girl!"

"It has, Jacob, it has."

"You oughta get yourself back here and prep for the classic. Show them young upstarts a thing or two about real riding."

Alex smiled at him. After she'd graduated from Athena, she'd done well in the annual Middleburg Classic charity horse show each time she was able to get that September weekend free to enter. In fact, for a while she had considered trying for the Olympic equestrian team. After a lot of thought she'd decided not to, for fear the extreme pressure would take the joy out of what she loved best— belting over a cross-country course with a horse she knew well, creating a team of human and animal unmatched in any other sport.

"I'm sure their horses will teach them everything they need to know," Alex said. And it was true. More than one rider who thought they knew it all had come to grief when they came across a horse who knew more. "Grandfather said Twill needed some work?"

"Oh, good, you take that nag out and run him ragged. Save me a lot of misery trying to deal with him when he's in one of his moods like he's been lately."

Alex laughed. Twill was a wonderful horse, but he had a mind of his own at times, and it took a strong hand to deal with him then. "I'll do that. I'm in a mood of my own."

But her mood had lifted. It was nearly impossible for her to stay down when she set foot in this world she loved.

"I'll get him for you. Want me to tack him up?"

Jacob always asked, and Alex always declined. It was part of the etiquette, and she barely noticed after all these years.

"I'll get your saddle, at least," Jacob insisted, and Alex let him. "You want the hunt seat?"

She nodded. After he had led out the big sixteen-and-a-half-hand blood bay and draped the bridle over the saddle on the rack next to the crossties he clipped the horse to, Alex thanked him and took over.

Twill was already groomed, but she took a brush and ran it over him anyway, talking to him the whole time. She'd ridden the horse often, but it had been a while and it never hurt to renew the acquaintance slowly.

Twill seemed cheerful enough today, taking the bit almost eagerly when she bridled him. Moments later they were trotting out of the stable. She took him into the big outside arena and let him warm up slowly. When he started tossing his head, ready for more, she sidled him up to the gate, made him restrain himself and sidestep it open like a gentleman, then closed it behind them.

When she turned him toward the start of the course, his ears shot forward, then back, as if asking, "Really? Really?"

"Yes," she told him sweetly, "we're going to run that mood right out of you."

He snorted and began the eager dance that told her he was ready to run, if she'd only turn him loose. The bay knew this course as well as she did, and she knew it backward, forward and from any point in the middle.

It was going to be just what she needed, she thought. She gathered herself, leaned forward slightly, settled her heels down in the stirrups.

"Now!"

The horse shot forward, building up speed as they tore down the long, gradual hill. She let him go, only beginning to gather him in when they made the turn that would lead to the first fences, three simple post and rails one after the other, to set the rhythm. Next would be the hedge, then the sharp turn and the race through the trees to the big fallen oak, one of the biggest jumps on the course. Then the stream, the wooden bridge and into the upper pasture with its own unique obstacle course. There were thirty jumps over ten miles of trail, a bit short of the Olympics, but still a good test and workout for horse and rider.

With the first powerful leap, Alex felt her heart take flight with the surging animal, and for now, she thought of nothing but the course, the whip of the air in her face, and the thousand pounds of pure muscle beneath her. Twill, bless him, never put a foot wrong, and although it was an effort to rein him in when she had to to set him up for the more difficult jumps, they made it through without a fault.

By the time they were done, Twill was tired but still willing to go. With a horse like this one, all heart, the rider had to be the guide. If you didn't stop him, he'd literally kill himself for you. She untacked the horse and gave him lots of congratulations and pats. This time when Jacob approached and offered to do the cool down and clean up, Alex glanced at her watch and reluctantly agreed.

"Only because I have to get to work sometime today," she said, and Jacob grinned at her.

"I know, girl. You take care of your own. But this time, let me help out. Make me feel useful."

Impulsively she gave the wiry man a hug. Jacob had been part of her life since she'd been born and she'd often felt more comfortable down here with him, especially if her mother had been around.

She ran back to the big house in a much lighter frame of mind. She showered hastily, dried herself and her hair, her body still humming with exhilaration. She'd needed that. Badly, she thought as she dressed.

She was on her way to work ten minutes later, leaving an understanding grandfather and a still bemused brother in her wake.

Chapter 8

"So he is FBI?" Alex asked. She'd run the prints she'd gotten from the filing cabinet and come up with a name—Justin Cohen, bona fide FBI agent.

"He's one of us, all right," her friend Sheila replied. "Has been for nearly ten years, one of those right out of college recruits. Now special agent assigned to the Phoenix field office."

Alex sat back in the office chair, thinking.

"He was part of the task force that broke up that alien-smuggling ring down there a while back," Sheila added. "It was all over the news. Lots of good PR for the bureau."

Fair-haired boy, Alex thought. Except his was nearly black. And those eyes...

She yanked her thoughts back to what was important right now. "What's he on now? Could you find out?"

"I thought you might want to know, so I asked. He's assigned to a possible receiving-and-fencing stolen property case now."

"Stolen property?" Alex asked, knowing that wasn't something that normally fell under the FBI's purview. "What's the twist?"

"They think they're hiding it out on the Gila River Indian Reservation."

"Guess that makes it ours, then," Alex said. Interesting, she added to herself. The border of the Gila River reservation was barely forty or fifty miles from Athena. Could someone be running stolen items through the school? That didn't make any sense, unless Rainy were somehow involved. And that made no sense at all.

"Oh, one more thing and then I've got to run, I have to pick Steven up from his soccer game," Sheila said. "My friend I talked to out there asked if he was in trouble."

"Cohen?"

"Yep. Said he'd been taking a lot of personal time off recently."

"Hmm," Alex said. "What did you tell her?"

"I told her not that I knew of. I didn't figure you'd want him to know, so I hinted that somebody here at headquarters had personal reasons for wanting to know, like she had the hots for him or something. Judging by his ID photo, it's likely true of somebody."

"Oh, he's a looker, all right," Alex said wryly. "Do me a favor and keep digging, will you? Anything you can find."

So, she thought after she'd hung up, he was assigned to a case centered close to Athena, but apparently unconnected to the school. And he'd been taking time off.

Could he be investigating Athena officially, but in an undercover capacity? That was a possibility. But why? Did someone else think there was something suspicious about Rainy's death? But that made no sense. Even if someone did suspect, the FBI would have no jurisdiction. Unless there was even more involved here than the Cassandras suspected.

Alex shook her head sharply. She felt like she was slogging through a swamp, with things pulling at her from all sides, some poisonous, some just trying to drown her. She wanted all of these questions answered, but they were incidental. The real bottom line was simple, she told herself, and all the other stuff was secondary. Was Justin Cohen one of the good guys or one of the bad guys?

It was a question she couldn't answer right now, and she'd learned long ago not to waste energy on such things. She would stay alert and gather more information whenever she could. But right now she needed to clear up the things that had piled up in her absence so she could get back to her personal investigation.

I have to pick Steven up from his soccer game....

She'd heard Sheila say it a dozen times a month

over the years. Steven this, Steven that. Her eight-year-old son was her pride, her joy, practically her life. Alex had never quite understood the bond between them, but had figured she would when she had children of her own someday.

Children of her own.

A chill swept through her. Her entire vision of her future was rattled, maybe destroyed. Would it ever happen? Or had the choice really been taken away from her, like it had been for Rainy?

Easy, there, you're making an awful lot of assumptions, she told herself. You're not certain exactly what happened to Rainy, and you have no idea that anything at all happened to you. Chill.

Her phone rang, and she was grateful for the interruption of thoughts that shook her way down deep. She wasn't used to her emotions being out of control, but she seemed to have lost the knack of controlling them the moment she'd learned about Rainy, and it was getting worse every minute.

"Forsythe," she said into the receiver.

"Hello, Alexandra."

"Emerson," she said. "I was going to call you this evening to let you know I was back in town."

"And going to stay this time, I hope?"

"I'm not sure how long. There are…things I still have to handle in Arizona, and I don't know yet when the funeral will be. Soon, though."

"I see." He said it calmly, ever patient. "Shall we have dinner this evening?"

"Can you, on such short notice?" He was usually as busy as she was, sometimes more. Whenever they went out they both turned off their cell phones, but that only made it a toss-up as to whose pager would go off first.

"Everything is under control at the moment. I've made my last rounds, and everyone appears to be stable."

"All right."

"Seven?"

"Make it eight. I've got a lot of catching up left to do here."

"Fine. Eiffels?"

"I'd rather do Fran O'Brien's, if you don't mind. I'm hungry for one of their steaks."

"How carnivorous of you. But if you must."

She knew he hated the football-themed restaurant, but they served the best steaks around. She stifled the urge to tell him to get his nose lowered. She knew she was running short on patience in just about every area right now, so she tried to be extra careful. And she did want to see him, talk to him. He was so calm, so controlled, that just being with him might help her get a handle on these unaccustomed emotions.

"I'll meet you there," she said.

She turned her attention back to her desk and began to plow through reports. The paperwork had been the hardest thing to get used to—she was used to doing. It was only because of years of strictly imposed self-discipline that she was able to focus on the work at hand and not let her mind skitter back to the all-consuming matter of Rainy's death.

Every one of these people, she lectured herself, probably left people behind who are now feeling just like you feel with Rainy gone. Remember that, and give them your best.

It was still warm when she finally left the office, but it would cool a little throughout the evening. And soon, she thought, glancing in the direction of the academy, the trees would start to turn, and Quantico would put on its fall dress of gorgeously colored leaves.

And Rainy would still be dead.

At five to eight—Alex was never one to be late, nor to play the game of keeping a man waiting— she arrived at the lower level of the Capitol Hilton and walked into the restaurant named after the former Washington Redskins tackle.

"Ms. Forsythe, welcome!"

"Thank you, Candace," Alex told the hostess who had seen her here often with her grandfather, less often with Emerson. "Is Mr. Howland already here?"

"Yes, I'll take you to the table."

With the good manners that were inbred in him, Emerson stood up as she approached. A smile warmed his face, the same smile that had drawn her to him in the first place. She was still amazed at how it changed his usually solemn expression.

"You look lovely, as always," he said, giving her a welcoming embrace.

"You're looking dapper yourself."

He always looked well, with his well-cut blond hair and regular features, but he was wearing the dark blue suit she'd helped him pick out just before she'd gotten the call from Rainy. She was touched that he'd thought to wear it tonight.

"A lady of excellent taste selected it," he said as she took the chair he held for her.

"The lady thanks you," she said.

She felt herself beginning to unwind. Emerson's presence was always soothing, she guessed it was part of what made him such an excellent doctor. And it was a calm she needed just now, more than ever.

An expert at small talk, probably because of the necessity for a facile bedside manner, Emerson carried the conversation easily through the ordering of dinner and wine. As he chatted about what had been happening with people they knew while she'd been gone, Alex wondered suddenly what kind of doctor he would be dropped in a small town like Eloy, where Rainy had died. For an acclaimed physician who had spent his entire life on the heavily populated eastern seaboard, the idea of a small, isolated town of merely ten thousand population would probably be stultifying. Especially when he thrived on the adulation of the medical community.

Not, Alex reminded herself, that he didn't deserve it. The man quite literally saved lives by the dozen. It was one of the things that had made her say yes when, after they'd met at one of those social functions she'd grown to dislike, he'd called and asked her to dinner.

She knew she was distracted, but it was brought home to her sharply just how distracted by his reaction when the question that had been bubbling up inside her finally popped free.

"Do you want children, Emerson?"

He blinked. "I beg your pardon?"

They had mentioned it in passing when they'd become officially engaged, but it had been in that general, far off, someday kind of way. Now it had suddenly become urgent.

"It's something we should talk about more seriously, don't you think?"

His mouth twisted into a wry grimace. "Quite. I just hadn't expected you to bring it up in the middle of a discussion about new open-heart procedures."

"Oh."

She felt herself start to flush, and lowered her head to hide it. She obviously hadn't heard a word he'd been saying on the subject, since she'd had no idea that was what he'd been talking about.

"It's all right, Alexandra. I know you're a bit muddled right now."

She half expected him to reach out and pat her hand. If he had, she wasn't sure she could have kept herself from biting it. Emerson's patience was sweetly endless, but also a bit condescending at times.

She shoved those thoughts aside and repeated her question, adding, "I mean really want children, want to be a father, not just feel it's your job to contribute the next generation of Howlands to the world."

Something about the flicker in his eyes hinted that she'd hit exactly the right—or wrong—nerve. Was that how he felt? She knew his parents had been pushing him to marry and reproduce, and had long suspected it wasn't out of the desire to cuddle grandchildren. The Howland name was old and respected, nearly as much as the Forsythe name, and both his parents had been delighted at the thought of melding the two families. It seemed a match made in heaven. And if Alex now and then suspected it would also be heralded on Wall Street and by the DAR, she tried not to let it bother her.

"Of course," Emerson finally said, long after the quick gut reaction she would have preferred, "I wish to have children. I look forward to raising them, molding them. I'd like to think I—we—could contribute finely-raised, educated and worthwhile members of society."

Nothing wrong with the sentiment, Alex thought. So why was her first thought that he sounded like a pompous bore? What was wrong with her? She had never been so critical of Emerson before. He'd never set her so on edge, made her wish he would simply let his hair down, skip shaving on a weekend, put on sweats to go somewhere other than just the gym where he kept in tip-top shape, pointing out that performing hours-long heart operations was no job for the weak in body or mind.

"Personally," she said, unable to stop herself, "I look forward to summers at the farm, teaching them about hoof picks and shoveling manure."

"Equestrian pursuits are acceptable," he said with a nod.

If she'd hoped to rattle him, she obviously hadn't succeeded. And why, she wondered, did she want to rattle him at all? Was it simply that she wanted to pierce that unflappable exterior?

She dropped the subject, and Emerson reverted to exactly where he'd been in conversation before she had interrupted him as if she had never brought it up. Alex let him, although she barely tuned in. She was too busy trying to figure out her own motivations.

It made no sense, she thought as their meal arrived, that she would want to shake him up. Hadn't she wanted that very calm she'd been trying to shatter? Hadn't she come tonight in part because she hoped his unruffled demeanor would somehow rub off and calm her own tumultuous emotions?

She took a bite of her steak, then another, found it excellent as always, but somehow she wasn't enjoying it as much as usual. Odd, she thought, how she'd always resented people who judged her as being cool and aloof without even knowing her, but now she was trying desperately to be just that. And failing miserably.

"—for the children's sake."

She stopped chewing midbite, Emerson's last words echoing in her head and telling her she should have been paying more attention.

"Excuse me?"

Patiently, he repeated himself. "I said I will be glad when we do have them, and you turn to more suitable activities for the children's sake."

She stifled the urge to say "Excuse me?" again, in an entirely different tone of voice. "I'm not sure I understand what you mean," she said instead, taking care to keep her tone neutral.

"Of course I mean your work. It's certainly no job for a mother to have."

She knew she was gaping at him, but she couldn't help it. "Are you trying to tell me you would expect me to abandon my career?"

"Well, you certainly wouldn't want to bring such work home to a family, would you? I find the gruesome details repugnant, so a child could likely be traumatized."

I've not given you half the gruesome details on any case, Alex thought.

"I'm curious," she said, hanging on to that even tone with a great effort. "How can a man who makes his living cutting into living, breathing human bodies find my work gruesome?"

"My work is saving lives," he said simply. "Yours is dealing with messy, ugly deaths."

He had a point, she had to admit. But she felt compelled to point out, "Not always."

"Perhaps not. But it is often about crime and evil."

"And putting a stop to it," she pointed out.

"Yes. That is what makes it bearable. For now."

"I see." She took a deep breath to steady herself. "And what exactly is it you see me doing, when that time comes?"

"Whatever you wish, of course. If you feel you have to stay with the Bureau, surely you could transfer to a different part of the agency? Something…tidier?"

Ah, yes. Emerson would always want a tidy life. Orderly.

"What I do," she said carefully, "is help bring order back to chaos. Sort out chaos so life can become…tidy, if you must use that word, again."

He looked at her with a thoughtful expression for a silent moment or two. "I hadn't thought of it in quite that way before," he admitted. "And I do see your point."

She had to give him that, if you made your point validly, he would always acknowledge it. Still, she couldn't help thinking in this case it was grudging.

"But?" she prodded when he didn't go on.

He lifted a brow at her. "But nothing. There's no need to become defensive. I'm processing what you've said, Alexandra."

She flushed again, aware that he was right, she had reacted defensively. She had felt under attack. But she knew Emerson took his own time to reach a conclusion, and thus when he did, it was nearly unshakable.

"You seem…uncommonly confrontational to-night," he said. "Is there something else wrong? Besides your friend?"

She supposed she should be glad that the man she was engaged to was perceptive enough to deduce that. Many weren't. She took in a very long, deep breath, held it for a few seconds, then let it out slowly.

"It's all tangled up together," she said, certain now she wasn't ready to talk about her suspicions and what had led her to ask the question about children in the first place. And it was the truth; it was all intertwined. She just didn't have all the threads yet. Or the pattern they were woven into.

After dinner Emerson ordered her a tiramisu without asking, but since it was her favorite dessert here she decided she was pleased, not upset that he hadn't asked her about it this time.

"My parents have proposed that you, your mother and Charles come to the house for a planning session soon," he said over his last cup of espresso.

"Planning session?"

"Yes." He waved his hand—that long-fingered, dexterous surgeon's hand she loved—rather vaguely. "Picking the site for the ceremony, the reception, the guest list and all those other details."

"Oh. Isn't it a bit early? We haven't even set a date yet."

"When you're dealing with a wedding of this size, it's never too early, my mother says."

"This size?" Alex tried not to cringe; she'd attended many society weddings in her life, including some within the family, that had hundreds of guests. She had been hoping for something much smaller, simpler.

"She estimates that between your family's guest list and ours, we're looking at upwards of a thousand people, if not more. It will be the social event of the year."

He looked pleased. Alex felt a bit sick.

"She'll want to give you suggestions on your dress," Emerson said. "Please, just let her prattle on. Then you can do what you want."

What she wanted was to trot into the nearest Saks and pick something off the rack that she liked and that happened to be white or something close. The idea of cramming fittings like the ones her cousin Charlene had gone through into her already impossible schedule added to her queasiness about the whole thing.

"I've never seen your mother so happy," Emerson said. "She's so delighted our families will be connected officially."

The bite of tiramisu she'd just taken seemed to turn to chalk in her mouth. A snippet of conversation flashed through her mind, from the day she had told her mother Emerson had proposed and she had accepted.

"Wonderful!" her mother had exclaimed with no small amount of triumph. "The Howlands and the Forsythes. The perfect connection. Finally!"

Not a word about whether she loved him, was happy herself or even congratulations. Just the acknowledgment that the joining of two such prominent families was a delight to the socially conscious Veronica Forsythe. Alex had finally, years after she had given up even trying, pleased her mother.

Was that why she was doing it?

The question leaped into her mind, and she cringed at the impact it had. For a moment she stared at Emerson, wondering if that's what he was, the trophy presented to her mother, to prove she really was the good girl Veronica Forsythe had always wanted, and not the changeling who continually disappointed her by being more her grandfather's ideal than her mother's.

She also wondered, for the first time, if her grandfather had had to fight her mother to get her to allow Alex to attend Athena. Veronica rarely stood up to anyone. She usually relied on manipulation to get what she wanted. But she hadn't been able to manipulate Charles. Alex knew her mother hadn't liked the idea of her going, knew that the kind of woman Athena produced was far from her mother's vision of what a woman should be, but if there had been any arguing it had been done out of her presence.

"...favorite designer, although she agrees that if you prefer Wang or perhaps a European designer, that would be acceptable."

Alex belatedly tuned in again. Emerson continued. Her fiancé, she realized, was discussing wedding dress designers.

Suddenly it all seemed to be too much. All this urbane refinement layered over the shock and horror of Rainy's death made her more than a little ill. Abruptly she got to her feet.

"I'm sorry Emerson. I don't feel well. I'll call you."

She gave him a light kiss that landed more or less on his temple and then left him sitting there, at last showing emotion through a slightly stunned look on his face. And she was too agitated to appreciate the tiny victory.

Chapter 9

Alex wished now she'd never used that particular example to poke at Emerson. Because now that she had, the image of herself at the farm with a couple of kids, teaching them about the joy of horses, even while shoveling manure, wouldn't leave her alone.

She looked out the airplane window at the heart of America passing beneath her as she flew westward, but that image was all she saw. It grew clearer and clearer, until she almost ached with the power of it. And now she didn't know if it would ever come true. If it ever could come true.

That's why, of course, she realized. If it weren't for the suddenly very real possibility that it might never happen, that the choice to make it happen might have been stolen from her, it wouldn't be pressuring her so much. She'd never really worried about it, or even thought about it all that much until she'd had to consider someone else might have made that very personal choice for her, some total stranger who had no right to interfere, who moved by stealth and deception, who committed this awful violation in secrecy and left the horrible results to be discovered years later. It was—

She stopped herself. You can't do anything about it now. At this moment, on this plane, the only thing you can do anything about is your work. So do it.

She pulled the folder that held a printout of the one case she hadn't yet finished her report on out of her large bag. She'd brought it intending to finish it on this flight, but now she was beginning to doubt she'd ever be able to concentrate enough.

Focus, she ordered herself. Those little girls who were raped and murdered and dumped in drainage ditches deserve it. The photos of those tiny, broken bodies drove her, and she was finally able to get through the outline of the report she would finish inputting when she was able to get online with her laptop. She went through it all again, just to be sure. Her brick of evidence had to be solid, or the entire case could wash away and an animal with a vicious taste for young, innocent flesh could walk free again, the worst kind of predator.

When she was certain she'd done all she could,

she put the file away and locked that section of her satchel. She looked out the window of the airplane again. She finally gave up trying to distract herself and surrendered to the demanding thoughts of the mess she was heading back to.

The funeral tomorrow would be a painful, aching thing for all of them, probably especially for Josie who was on temporary duty out of the country and couldn't be there.

It didn't seem possible the Cassandras were burying one of their own. But she better than any of them knew it was true; there was nothing like an autopsy to convince you.

Rainy's death had pounded home to Alex that she herself could not count on the fifty or sixty years she'd always assumed she would have. A foolish assumption, probably, given that she dealt with the fallout from untimely death all the time, but there it was. Her intellect knew no one could count on that kind of generosity from life, but her gut shied away from that truth.

Was it a sign of maturity, this outgrowing of the youthful assumption of immortality? Or had it simply been scared out of her by Rainy's death? Would she lose it as time dulled the pain slightly? Would she go back to believing that people who died were of her grandfather's generation, or in some cases her mother's, but not her own? Never her own. Not yet.

But it had happened. It could happen again. And the fact that she had never expected it, despite the dangerous career paths many Athenans had taken, only made her feel naive and a bit stupid.

She wished she were as tired as she'd been on her last cross-country flight, so that she could sleep. But she'd slept so well at the farm, and surprisingly well the couple of days she'd had at home, she felt rested. If she'd thought about it a bit more, she would have stayed up later last night working for just this reason, to tire herself out. But she hadn't and therefore she had nothing to do but think. When they finally began the descent into Phoenix, she was more relieved than she wanted to admit. At least she could fill her head with the logistics of the rest of the trip, distract herself with the details of gates and baggage and rental cars.

The landing was as rough as her thoughts had been. The plane bounced and shook going through waves of rising heat. For a moment the irony of dying in a crash landing just minutes after her unpleasant earlier thoughts about death and funeral plans rolled over her until the plane finally settled safely on the ground.

She picked up her rental car, worked her way out of Sky Harbor airport onto Interstate 10, and headed north, then west. She had made plans to stay at Athena Academy tonight and go with Christine to Tucson for the funeral tomorrow. She was able to give enough attention to her driving to keep her thoughts out of what were rapidly becoming a pair of well-worn ruts. Between her suspicions about Rainy and her fears about what might have been done to her, as well, too much of her mind was running constantly hard and fast as it tried to sort, refute, prove and fill in too many blanks with too little information.

Maybe one of the others would have something by now. Maybe Kayla had turned up something more, or Christine. Anything that would make sense of this, anything that would turn this world of crazy theories and wild ideas into something reasonable and sensible.

But no matter what they might have learned, there couldn't be anything that would make Rainy's death acceptable. And that was the bottom line.

The funeral was going to be small for someone as well-loved as Rainy, but Alex thought it would be exactly what she would want, only those dearest to her to witness the end of her far too short life. Odd, that with everything the Cassandras talked about, they'd never talked much about death. At least, not in anything but the abstract.

They'd especially never talked about the death of one of their number. Once one of them had joked about the Vikings having the right idea, to go out on the water in a blaze of glory, but they'd never gone any further than that. More of that youthful belief in their own immortality, she supposed. But now here they all were, headed for a funeral, with no choice but to face the inevitability and finality of it.

Kayla had said she would go early to pick Darcy

up from the Tucson airport. Darcy would likely have her young son in tow. She never seemed to go anywhere without him.

Tory had called Christine last night to say she'd be there. Alex knew Tory had been covering a story in Britain, but suspected she would have been here even had the story not been finished. She hadn't made it to that first fateful meeting that Rainy had called, when Alex, Kayla, Darcy, Josie, and Christine had learned of Rainy's accident and then her death. Only Josie, unable to get leave, and Sam—who also had not made that meeting and who was God knows where on God knows what assignment for her employer, the CIA—would not be there. They weren't even sure their message about Rainy's death had reached her.

But though Josie and Sam would be absent in body, Alex knew they would be here in spirit. Even Sam. Because if Samantha St. John somehow knew, despite being out of reach, that Rainy was being buried today, Alex wouldn't be a bit surprised. Sam had a way of finding things out, her brilliant ability to hack just about any computer on the planet just one of her methods.

Alex had offered to drive her rental to Tucson, and Christine had accepted. Although she hadn't planned it that way, it occurred to her that this sad journey was the perfect chance to ask about what her grandfather had told her at the farm that night.

"I was able to visit my grandfather while I was back home," she said.

Christine turned to look at her and smiled warmly. "How is Charles? I haven't spoken to him in some time, I'm afraid. I keep meaning to call and catch up, but time always seems to get away."

"He understands," Alex assured the woman. "He knows what a huge job running Athena is. He's just glad you're here to do it. He even commented on the excellent job you do screening the staff."

Christine's smile widened. "That's good of him. We're lucky to have him as such a staunch supporter."

Alex negotiated a lane change to get out from behind a slow-moving truck. When she was safely in front, she changed back. She'd found herself driving very carefully of late.

"We were also talking about Rainy," she said when the maneuver was complete. "I asked him if there was anyone he could think of that could be holding a grudge they might take out on her."

"I'd find that hard to believe. She was such a lovely woman."

"I can't imagine it, either. But what if she were just…handy?" Alex glanced at her passenger. "What if the grudge was really against Athena?"

Christine drew back, obviously startled. Kayla clearly hadn't voiced her suspicions to Christine when Alex left. She turned her attention back to the road

"Athena? You think her death is connected to Athena?"

"I think it's possible. This isn't the first time someone connected to Athena has died mysteriously," Alex said, referring to the unsolved murder of Athena founder Marion Gracelyn nine years ago. "Many of us are in a position to keep our connection to Athena quiet, known only to those who have to know. But with Rainy it's a matter of public record, in her qualifications at the law firm, for anyone who bothers to look."

Christine's tone sounded thoughtful. "I suppose it's a possibility. We do have our enemies. People can be very resistant to change. There are people who fought Athena from its inception."

"What about after that?"

"After?"

"Has anybody been fired who could hold a grudge?"

"A disgruntled ex-employee? I don't think we've had any. Most who have left have gone by choice, for personal reasons or because they realized they weren't right for the job, or it wasn't right for them."

"You can't think of anyone who might feel they were treated unfairly?"

"And who would be angry enough to take revenge on a former student? No."

Alex waited until they had reached a straight, relatively clear section of road before she glanced at Christine again and asked, "What about Dr. Bradford?"

Christine's eyes widened, and to Alex's amazement she thought she saw a tinge of color rise in the woman's cheeks. Christine turned her head, almost jerkily, to look out the windshield.

Oh, boy, Alex thought, turning her eyes back to the road again herself. That hit a nerve.

"Oh, that was long, long ago," Christine finally said. "Back in our second year. Rainy was an eighth grader. But I'm sure there's no connection."

Christine seemed to have herself back in hand now, but Alex couldn't help wondering what had caused the uncharacteristic reaction.

"Who was he?"

"He is—at least I assume he still is—a doctor and researcher in behavioral science. He has focused most of his work on women, which is obviously unusual. That's why we thought he might be a good fit at Athena. But he wasn't full-time staff. He came as a guest lecturer for special psychology segments."

Alex stayed silent as she took the off-ramp they needed to get to the church. At the bottom was a traffic signal, with three cars backed up ahead of them. She eased the rental to a stop. Then she looked at Christine once more.

"What happened?"

There was a moment of silence before Christine answered. "He was…there was a problem between him and Betsy Stone."

Alex barely managed not to say that didn't surprise her. Betsy could inspire people to be difficult. She was a talented and competent nurse, but her bedside manner was not her strong suit.

But her grandfather had given her the impression the problem with Dr. Bradford had been with Christine herself, so she pressed on.

"A problem?"

"He was…harassing her. So I recommended that he not be asked back."

Alex found it a little hard to believe that anyone would dare harass the formidable Betsy Stone, but she was distracted from that thought by the realization that the usually serene, unflappable Christine seemed to be having trouble looking her in the eye as she spoke.

Chapter 10

Alex had expected Allison Gracelyn at the funeral and wasn't surprised to see her already there when she and Christine pulled into the parking lot of the small chapel. Not only was Allison an Athena Academy board consultant, but she had been in Rainy's class and one of Rainy's closest friends besides the Cassandras.

She was now an NSA programmer and mathematician. But she was also the daughter of late Athena founder Marion Gracelyn, who had died tragically from a blow to the head right there at Athena. The first time death had visited. Though it had been suspected that her death was not accidental, motive and a murderer had never been found. Marion had been the woman who had had the vision, who had made the dream of Athena come true. This made Alex feel a kinship with Allison, along with fellow Cassandra Josie Lockworth, whose father had been not only an early and strong supporter of Athena but who had also been director of the CIA at the time of its inception. They had all had exceptionally large footsteps to follow in at Athena, and they had all felt the strain of the effort.

Allison's brother, David, was with her. The two looked much alike, with their dark brown eyes and hair, and were easily recognizable as siblings.

Alex's brow furrowed as she watched Allison whisper something to her brother, to which he shook his head. His jaw was tightly clenched, she saw, his feelings obviously very near the surface. He even moved somewhat jerkily, like a man on the emotional edge, or running on nerves alone. She recognized the symptoms all too well.

Then she had to concentrate on parking the car. As she got out and turned to lock the door, she saw Kayla walking toward the church with another brunette, a short-haired woman who had a child in tow. She frowned. The child was Darcy's adorable little Charlie, she'd seen them both a little more than a week ago, but….

She looked a second time at the woman who was holding the boy's hand. The change in Darcy Allen Steele was still a shock.

But once she looked past the dyed brown hair, and

blue eyes made brown by what had to be colored contact lenses, it was clearly Darcy Allen. Bright, eager-to-please Darcy, who had always excelled at disguise. She had once made redheaded, fair-skinned Alex look like a dark-eyed, honey-skinned Latina, and won the drama class trophy when nobody could guess who was under the dark wig.

They hadn't had time to talk about Darcy's situation the night Rainy died. Alex supposed she would get answers later. She was certain Darcy had good reasons for whatever she was up to. Right now, she needed to get inside, the service would be starting shortly.

The small chapel was reminiscent of Greek architecture, complete with columns. It was elegant and classical, strong and graceful, just as Rainy herself had been, and it seemed to Alex the perfect place for this, her final send-off.

Christine went ahead to speak to Marshall Carrington as the official representative of Athena. Despite her determination to get through this, Alex found herself lingering outside, putting off going in as if that would somehow change things. As if once she stepped inside, once she saw that coffin there would be no further denial, no avoiding the fact that it was really time to say goodbye.

Finally she stepped inside. It was blessedly cool and seemed dim after the desert sun. She pulled off her sunglasses, although she wished she could keep them on; crying was something she allowed herself so rarely she had never quite gotten the hang of doing it with any kind of grace. But at the moment she didn't care, about grace or tears or anything else. There was no room for anything inside her except a wrenching, huge sense of loss.

Many of the people inside she recognized, including Rainy's parents, who lived in California where Rainy had grown up. Alex had met them a few times in her first year at Athena. Some people she didn't know, but was able to guess from her knowledge of Rainy who they likely were. Down in front on the left, directly behind Marshall, she saw Kayla and the almost unrecognizable Darcy, with the child on her lap. As she looked, Kayla glanced back and saw her. A moment later, as if she'd had to think about it, she leaned over and whispered something to Darcy, then they both slid over on the pew, leaving room for one more person on the end.

Alex hesitated. Had Kayla had to think about whether she wanted her there, or had she simply not been sure Alex would accept the silent offer?

Does it really matter? Isn't this the right time to get this behind us? What if it had been she herself, or Kayla, who had died and left this breach between them?

Alex knew it was time. And so, mindful that this was likely the best gift she could give Rainy, she walked down to that pew and sat beside the woman who had once been her best friend. Kayla didn't look at her, but Alex thought she sensed her relaxing, as if her body had been tensed as she waited for Alex to decide. It wasn't much, but it was a start.

In the last moments before the service began, there was a flurry of activity at the back of the chapel. Everyone turned to look. Despite her grief, Alex smothered a smile as Tory entered in a rush, her chin-length black hair tousled, as if she'd just rushed in straight from the airport, which she probably had. Tory just seemed to have that effect, whenever she went anywhere people turned to look. And they had done so even before her face had become famous. She never demanded it, never expected it, it just happened.

Alex was certain many of the mourners recognized the well-known network news reporter, and the murmur that circled the room seemed to prove that. Tory glanced around, her gaze stopping here and there as if on familiar faces. But then she realized they'd been about to start, and quickly took a seat in the back.

The minister began to speak, in that generic way of someone who hadn't really known the person that well. The few personal references had likely been supplied by Marshall, or perhaps Kayla during the arrangements for this service. Rainy's father spoke, then Marshall, both bringing tears to the eyes of the mourners, and some smiles as they recalled happy memories.

Alex hadn't thought of speaking herself. When they reached the point at which the minister asked if anyone else wished to speak, she glanced at

Kayla, who shook her head slightly, indicating with a small nod the back of Marshall's head and slumped shoulders. His speech seemed to have taken every reserve of his energy. Alex had noticed Kayla occasionally reaching forward to grip his shoulder comfortingly during the service.

Darcy wouldn't even meet her gaze. She glanced back toward Tory, the most likely one of them to be comfortable getting up in front of a group to speak. To her surprise, Tory also gave her a quick shake of the head, and then a slight gesture with her chin, as if pointing back at Alex.

She got the message.

You do it.

When she turned back, the minister was looking at her. After a moment, she nodded. Slowly, she got to her feet, wondering what on earth she would say. But when she got to the podium and turned to look out at the small gathering, the words just seemed to pour out.

"We all loved Rainy. She was a bright, talented, successful woman. But she was so much more. She was friend, mentor and, on occasion, mother-confessor. She was peacemaker and ringleader, and above all role model. She got saddled with a group of young, incredibly naive girls who had very little in common except strong personalities that seemed forever at odds with each other. She took those girls—"

Alex's voice broke, and she had to stop for a moment. She swallowed hard, fought back the tears that threatened. She saw Christine smile at her encouragingly, Darcy, too. And beside Darcy, Kayla nodded, as if to urge her to continue. Alex took a deep breath to steady herself, and began again.

"She took those girls and turned them, by hook, crook and whatever trick came to hand, into a team that went straight to the top. None of us would be where we are—or who we are—had we not had the great, great good fortune of having Rainy in our lives. And the hole she leaves behind is unfillable, the wound unhealable. But she would not want us to ache like this forever. I can hear her saying, the moment this service is over, 'All right, everyone, let's get on with it.'"

Alex saw smiles around the room, sad ones, wistful ones, trembling ones, as she used Rainy's favorite phrase for moving things along.

"We will miss her. Forever. There will never be another quite like her. But we who are left behind will go on, because that's what she would want. And for Rainy, we will do what needs to be done, no matter what it is, and we will do it in a way that would make her proud."

If she had sounded a bit vehement, she didn't care. If there had seemed to be a deeper meaning, all the better. If anyone in this room knew anything about what had happened, they stood warned. The Cassandras would find out what had happened, and whoever was responsible for this would pay.

* * *

"Thanks, Alex." Tory took her hand and squeezed it. "You did it beautifully."

"I thought you would—"

"I know. But I didn't want anything to detract from why we were here. And sometimes my presence has a weird effect on people."

Alex smiled at her fellow Cassandra as they stood in the small area just inside the doors of the chapel. They had all stopped on the way out to express their sympathy and grief to Marshall as well as Rainy's parents, then had gathered here. "It's your own fault, for becoming a big-shot reporter."

Tory grimaced, but her vivid green eyes twinkled. "Just like Rainy always said. 'You're such a ham, Victoria. You're going to end up a star, you wait and see.'"

Alex felt her eyes begin to brim at the recollection. "She had such faith in all of us…."

"We haven't let her down. And we won't. Even Kayla's pulled it out. She's solid as a rock now. I know Rainy was worried about her." Tory frowned slightly then. "But what's up with Darcy?"

"I'm not sure. I haven't had a chance to really talk with her." Darcy had disappeared immediately after the service had concluded, Alex guessed to calm down the child who had become fussy by the end of the service.

"How about you and Kayla?" Tory asked in the blunt manner she sometimes used in interviews with great success. "I saw you were sitting together."

Alex didn't pretend to misunderstand. "We're… working on it."

"Good. It's about time."

"We've all drifted apart," Alex said.

"I know we have. And I don't like it. Rainy didn't like it. So we'd better get us all back together, the way we're supposed to be."

"It'll never be the same," Alex said sadly.

"But it would be worse if we didn't do it, wouldn't it? If we let it all fall apart, after how hard Rainy worked to bring us together?"

"Of course," Alex agreed, Tory's brisk tone shaking her out of her misery. "And I need to talk to you. About what's been going on, I mean."

Tory smiled grimly. "I know. I didn't even get Rainy's message until after—after she died. I'm sorry I wasn't there with you all. Kayla's given me the basics. And I have to say I don't much care for what I've heard, but I know there has to be more."

"A lot. Something's going on, but I don't want to discuss it here. After the graveside ceremony, can we—"

"Alex?" She turned then, to see Kayla coming up behind her, followed by Darcy, her now quieted child in her arms. "What you said…that was lovely."

"Yes, it was," Darcy said, her voice very quiet and subdued.

"Thank you," Alex said to both of them, meaning it.

The two newcomers turned to greet Tory, and a round of hugs followed.

"Have you given her the latest yet?" Kayla asked Alex, indicating Tory.

"I was just suggesting we go someplace else to talk about it," Alex said, glancing around at the people slowly beginning to make their way out of the church.

"Good idea," Kayla agreed. "Let's get out of here."

Kayla led the way to the double doors and pulled them open. She was the only one who didn't react to the blast of heat from outside. It truly didn't take long to lose your acclimatization, Alex thought.

Kayla went down the steps still looking back at Alex and the others. "Why don't we—"

"Oh, God," Darcy said, going very still and staring out toward the parking lot.

The other three women turned to look. Alex saw the van with the satellite dish on the roof, and the network logo on the side. People were scurrying around it, setting up. She blinked. A TV crew? Here?

"Damn," Tory muttered under her breath. "It's ABS. You don't suppose…"

She leaned forward, peering around, eyes moving quickly as if she were searching for someone. Her darting gaze stopped, riveted on someone or something. Then she swore again, harsher this time.

"It is her."

"Who?" Kayla asked.

"Shannon Conner."

Alex whirled around. Except for occasional

glimpses on television she hadn't been able to avoid, she hadn't seen Shannon Conner since her expulsion from Athena. But here she was in the flesh, her shoulder-length blond hair perfectly coiffed, her face artfully drawn with TV makeup, her nails a dagger-tip shade of red as her fingers curled around the microphone she held. And in light of her conversation with G.C., Alex was even more suspicious.

Alex wondered if Allison had seen her yet. Like Rainy, her classmate Allison had been a mentor to a group of new Athena students. Allison's group had called themselves the Graces, and one of them had been Shannon Conner, who had literally fallen from grace. Alex had no idea if there was any relationship remaining between them, or anyone else from Athena for that matter. The woman had had a few friends, as she recalled, but whether they had stuck by her in her disgrace she didn't know. No one had seemed too upset by her abrupt departure. But Conner had landed on her feet, as her kind—smart and ruthless—often do.

Alex glanced at Tory. "I always suspected she went into TV reporting mainly to go after you."

Tory grimaced. "Sometimes I think so, too. I know she blames me for her humiliation."

"Never mind that it was her own actions, trying to frame Josie of all people for stealing, that brought it on her," Kayla said, her voice cold as she looked at the woman next to the satellite van.

"Maybe we should just go out another way,"

Darcy suggested, sounding anxious. "Get away from her."

Alex turned back to look at the fellow Cassandra she hadn't seen in so long. An Athena, run away? That was so unlike any of them, including Darcy, that Alex couldn't think of a thing to say. But there was no denying Darcy looked more than wary, she looked frightened. Her grip on her child tightened, until the boy squirmed in protest.

And then it was taken out of their hands.

"Uh-oh, she's spotted us," Tory muttered. "And here she comes. Okay, remember what you'll sound like to the uninformed. And beware of sound bites, she'll try and sucker you into one. Best course, say something totally unrelated to whatever she asks."

The blonde and two men, one with a large camera on his shoulder, the other seeming to be only holding a bunch of cables together, were walking purposefully toward them. There was no question of avoiding it now.

"Might as well find out what the…woman's up to," Alex said.

"Better now than later," Kayla agreed.

"The camera's already rolling," Tory warned them. "Assume the sound is live, too."

Darcy made a small sound, almost a whimper of protest, but Alex didn't have time to look at her. That Tory was right became obvious as Shannon Conner quickly came toward them, and when she got within hearing distance and they could see and hear she was already talking.

"—in certain exclusive, private, highly ranked government circles, the reputation of Athena Academy is well known," she was saying into the microphone. "It's not a place the average citizen is aware of, although perhaps they should be. Any place with this many connections to the military, and government activities both open and covert, should be under the watchful eye of the public."

So that's her plan, Alex thought. I should have known.

She felt the pump of adrenaline, as if she were gearing up for a fight. As, she supposed, she was. Conner turned to face them.

Here we go.

Chapter 11

The blonde had managed to negotiate the church stairs, snap orders at the cameraman, keep an eye on both the cables she was dodging and the women she was heading for, all without missing a step. Or a word as she continued.

"Where the Athena Academy gets its funding will be the topic of a later investigative segment, but today we will be speaking to several alumni of the supersecret prep school, gathered in Tucson today to mark the untimely passing of one of its most successful and publicly known graduates, attorney Lorraine Miller Carrington."

Alex wondered what the woman would do if they simply refused to acknowledge her. Probably make it into the lead story of the day, she answered her own question sourly. She could just hear it, spoken in tones guaranteed to blow things up into a huge drama, how the women of Athena had refused to speak, and what did they have to hide? No mention of their grief, of course, and how they simply might not want it aired for public consumption. Never that.

"Here we have Alexandra Forsythe, granddaughter of famed financier Charles Forsythe, well known in Washington D.C. power circles."

Oh, lucky me, I get to be first. But even as she thought it her mind was racing. She wouldn't let a bitter, jealous one-time rival rattle her, even if she did have a microphone in her hand, a television camera behind her and a nationwide audience.

"Since all the records are kept so well hidden," Conner was saying in a tone that hinted she knew exactly what those records contained, "and Forsythe has a bank of attorneys to shield him, it's not general knowledge how much he has contributed to the school to be on the board, but what is known is that his only granddaughter is a graduate."

Fuming inwardly at the provocative phrasing Conner was using, Alex nevertheless pasted the society smile she'd learned very early in life onto her face. Finally, all that Mayflower family, DAR stuff was going to come in handy. She might actually have to thank her mother before this was over.

"Why, hello," she said brightly, with her best blueblood, aristocratic smile. "Are you an advance scout for a TV station? Are we truly going to be on the local news?"

Her pretense of not knowing who Conner was, and her slight emphasis on the "local" hit their mark; Conner's lips thinned slightly and her next words were clipped.

"I'm a network reporter. This is national coverage. Tell me how you all felt when you discovered your friend had been the subject of scientific experiments while she was a student at Athena Academy? Is it true that even though there is absolutely no evidence, you now suspect she didn't die in an accident but rather was murdered?"

The bluntness of the question and the shock of realizing anyone outside their circle knowing anything about what they were looking into nearly stunned Alex. Even ignoring the continued purposeful phrasing that made the Athenans appear as if they were fantasizing a conspiracy because they couldn't accept their friend's death, she was shocked that Conner knew so much.

Or thought she knew, she corrected herself silently, remembering that throwing questions that implied knowledge was a typical ruse of reporters, and all too often it worked on innocent people who didn't suspect the ulterior motive.

Her practiced social smile held steady, never faltering as she made a production of turning to face the reporter and the camera. Best defense, she thought, and in an elaborate double take, she looked at Conner again.

"Wait, don't I know you from somewhere?"

"I told you, I'm a national network reporter."

"No, I've never seen you on television, it's…oh, I remember! You were the only person ever thrown out of Athena, for incompetence, lying and trying to frame an innocent student!"

That ought to get me edited out, Alex thought with satisfaction as she turned away from the still-running camera and clearly irritated reporter. But Alex could have sworn she saw the cameraman's mouth twitch, as if he were fighting a smile. After a moment to apparently get her temper in hand, the blonde zeroed in on Kayla.

"It may come as a surprise to the taxpaying citizens of Youngtown, Arizona, that one of their own police lieutenants is a product of a school they didn't even know existed. And more surprising, that she is assigned to the town of Athens, which came into existence solely to serve that covert school. But here is Lieutenant Kayla Ryan. Since she has no rich grandfather, indeed her family still lives on the Navajo reservation here in northeastern Arizona, she likely had to work a lot harder for her success. She—"

"Those who didn't want to work were weeded out early," Kayla said, the reference back to Alex's words about her being thrown out of Athena unmistakable.

There was no hiding Conner's growing anger now. "As a police lieutenant," she said, her tone sharp now, "do you have anything to say about the homicide that took place at Athena nearly a decade ago? Have there been more killings since Marion Gracelyn was murdered? Were they covered up? Do you suspect this death is related?"

Alex barely stopped herself from spinning on her heel and taking the woman out with a well-placed right cross; to hell with finesse, Conner deserved to be knocked on her ass. One glance at Kayla's face told her she was thinking along the same lines.

And Darcy was…gone.

Distracted, Alex's brow furrowed. She hadn't even noticed her departure. Maybe just as well, who knows what Conner would have done to her poor little boy. Before she could dwell upon the abrupt vanishing act, Tory had stepped in to put an end to the verbal fencing.

"My," she said smoothly, looking into the camera steadily, her manner as cool and polished as it was on her own broadcasts, "things must be run quite differently at ABS. At UBC they would never dream of assigning a reporter with such an obvious conflict of interest to a story."

The cameraman lifted his head from the viewfinder and looked at Conner, as if waiting for her to tell him to shut down. Tory went on speaking, and as was a news cameraman's instinct—and he was old enough to have been at it awhile—he kept on filming.

"Being the only person in the history of Athena to be thrown out, accused of a crime, and yet assigned to a story about the school? What an ethical dilemma! For someone who has any ethics, anyway. Of course, a person with ethics would immediately and properly turn that story over to someone else who could do it without bias."

"My story will be the truth!" Shannon burst out, losing her cool at last.

"Oh? Then you'll want to share with your viewers exactly how you knew to come here today. How did you find out when and where this service was, when no one outside Rainy Carrington's immediate family and closest friends knew?"

"None of your business."

Tory let the unprofessional response stand. "In fact, how did you even know Rainy was dead? It's certain no one from Athena told you."

Shannon Conner didn't miss the implied insult. She had been many things, most of them unpleasant, but she had never been stupid.

"I don't reveal my sources. Especially to you!" she snapped.

"So they're 'anonymous' sources, then?" Tory said putting so much biting emphasis on the word that Alex had to smother a grin.

Conner opened her mouth as if to retort angrily, and held it that way ungraciously for a long moment without speaking. Alex was about to make a comment about the number of cicadas that seemed to be buzzing around this year when the woman popped it shut again.

"Cut it," she snapped at the camera operator,

and turned her back on them and started toward the van. The cameraman pushed a couple of buttons, then looked at the group of women he'd been filming with interest. And with, Alex realized in surprise, a glint of approval in his eyes. And he gave them a broad wink before he turned to follow the fuming reporter down the steps.

"He's seen a few like her come and go," Tory said, echoing what Alex was thinking. Then she turned to the others, including Darcy, who had reappeared. "I took a cab from the airport. Can I hitch a ride to the cemetery with one of you?"

"Christine suggested that we all ride together," Alex said. "She said she'll bring my rental car. She thought we might want to catch up on… things."

"Good. We can all fit in my SUV," Kayla said.

"I'll just grab my bag. I dropped it off in the church office," Tory said, and headed back inside.

Moments later they were all loaded up in the blue SUV, Kayla behind the wheel, Alex in the front passenger seat, and Tory, Darcy and her little boy in the rear. Tory had said she wanted to sit with Charlie, Darcy's son. But since he had, in that perverse way children had, gone to sleep now that quiet was no longer necessary, Alex wondered about that. She wouldn't put it past Tory to maneuver things just so Alex would end up in front with Kayla.

But she said nothing, and let it be as they drove through Tucson to the cemetery. Rainy's ultimate destination.

* * *

There was something inexpressibly final about the sight of a casket hovering over a freshly dug grave. The sight of Marshall staring at the hole only pounded the fact home. This was the end of Rainy's journey, Alex thought. But it was just the beginning of theirs. They would, as Tory had said, find out what had really happened to their friend, inspiration and mentor. They were the Cassandras.

The sound of the cicadas here on the hillside nearly drowned out the minister's voice as he recited the service. Alex tried to listen, but it all seemed meaningless to her now, when she knew there was so much more to Rainy's death than they knew.

Yet.

She drew in a deep breath of the hot air, the scent of heated sage and mesquite filling her nostrils. Trying to assuage the ache inside the only way she could think of right now, she lifted her head to look across the bright green lawns toward the stark mountains that bordered Tucson. They looked similar to the White Tanks, rising behind Athena Academy. Appropriate.

Her gaze snapped back, searching for what she'd just glimpsed. She scanned the area across the lane that led into the cemetery, certain she'd seen something. Someone. Someone who looked familiar.

Someone who looked very much like the mysterious Justin Cohen.

He was gone. Or at least, she couldn't see him

anywhere near where she thought he'd been standing before. But she was almost certain it had been him. She'd certainly thought about him often enough since that day she'd surprised him in the infirmary.

Of course, what was not to think about? He was, as she'd told Sheila, definitely a looker.

But he was also FBI and had run to avoid telling anyone why he'd been on the Athena grounds. As far as she knew so far, not having heard any news from Sheila, he had no legitimate reason to be there. That told Alex she'd best assume he was not on their side.

It all continued to spin around in her mind. The minister was finished, and as each Cassandra filed by the grave to toss in the rose she held, Alex's thoughts were still racing. She stopped them with a conscious effort as she tossed in her own flower and with it a promise to the woman being buried that her sisters would never give up the search for what had really happened.

But as she moved on, her mind revved anew.

What would the FBI agent be doing here, now, at Rainy's graveside service? Had he been at the church, too, and she just hadn't seen him?

Sheila had said he was assigned to a receiving-and-fencing stolen property case, the FBI connection being the Gila River reservation possibly being the site of a clearing house for the operation. So why was he in Tucson at Rainy's service?

How had he known?

"Come on," Kayla said. "Let's go someplace where we can talk."

It was obvious that by that Kayla meant they should go somewhere where they could be alone and not overheard. Darcy picked up on it and quickly ran to Christine, apparently to ask her to keep an eye on Charlie. She handed over the boy and was back moments later.

They headed for a flat, open lawn area that had no gravesites yet. The openness ensured that no one would be listening. They'd see anyone who dared approach.

They settled down in a circle on the green grass, heedless of the toll on their funeral clothes. Quickly, Alex and Kayla brought the others up to date on what they'd discovered, including the mechanical scars on Rainy's ovaries and the fact that her emergency appendectomy all those years ago had been a fake. Alex filled them in on what Christine had said about Dr. Bradford and Betsy Stone, as well.

"There's more," Alex said, even though Tory and Darcy were staring at them in shock. "I caught an FBI agent snooping around Athena before I left last Wednesday."

Tory lifted a brow at her. "Do you guys 'snoop'?"

"I investigate," Alex said primly. "This guy snoops."

The moment of comic relief broke the tension.

"Do you know who he is?" Darcy asked.

"I checked on him. He's legit, out of the Phoenix office. But he's not on a case that has anything to do with Athena. And," she added, "I think I saw him today."

"Today?" Darcy sat up a little straighter.

Alex nodded. "Just now. At the graveside. I just caught a glimpse, so I can't be positive but…"

"You're positive," Tory said quietly.

Alex hesitated, then nodded. "Yes. Yes, I am. And I plan to do a lot more research on Agent Justin Cohen."

"Great. The feds," Kayla muttered, then blushed as she remembered her muttered epithet included two of her fellow Cassandras. "Sorry. You know what I mean."

"Yes," Alex said easily. "We use the same tone about 'locals'."

"Touché," Kayla acknowledged with a crooked smile. But her expression quickly changed back to serious as she went on. "Something else. I also discovered that Rainy had been researching egg mining. I found several files she'd downloaded from the Internet on her computer."

"Egg mining?" Darcy asked, her eyes widening. "You mean, like harvesting?"

Kayla nodded.

"Which would match with the scars I saw," Alex said, her voice tight and her expression grim. "And it would fit with Ms. Airhead Reporter's attack at the church."

"You think it happened way back when Rainy

supposedly had her appendix out? So long ago?" Tory asked.

"I just know it fits," Alex said. "With the scars, it makes perfect sense."

"So…instead of it being her appendix, they drugged her and stole her eggs?" Tory asked, this seeming a bit far-fetched even for a woman who dealt with outrageous stories as a matter of course.

"That's insane," Darcy whispered, glancing over her shoulder toward the still lingering mourners, where Christine was carrying her son away from the grim scene. "That would have to mean someone at Athena was involved, wouldn't it?"

"Yes," Kayla said, as Darcy reached the same conclusion she had.

"That's also insane. But none of this has been sane," Tory said, sounding for once thoroughly disheartened.

There was a long moment of silence. The cicadas buzzed, the desert heat beat down on them, yet they stayed there, taking it, as if it were some sort of ceremony beyond the one that had already taken place today. Alex could almost feel the bonds growing anew as if forged by the ferocious sun. The Cassandras were together again, and together they were unstoppable.

"What are the chances," Tory mused aloud, "that Rainy's murder—" She stopped as the others went very still. "That is what we're talking about, isn't it?"

"It is," Darcy said softly, hugging herself as if

she wasn't quite sure what to do with arms that weren't holding her child.

"Murder," Alex said softly, as if saying it aloud made it more real that just thinking it.

"What are the chances of what?" Kayla asked briskly, prodding them back to Tory's original statement.

"That this has nothing to do with Athena," Tory finished her statement.

All the Cassandras looked at each other, brows furrowing as they considered the possibility.

"I thought about that," Alex said. "I mean, I considered the possibility that I was hooking things together that didn't necessarily go together. It's a natural reaction, when something like this happens to someone like Rainy. You get to thinking everything that happens is somehow connected."

"Exactly. But she was an attorney, after all," Tory continued, "and since she's returned to Arizona she's dealt with some cases that cost some people."

"But not criminal," Darcy pointed out. It was true, Rainy had dealt mostly in corporate law.

"Sometimes the supposed noncriminals are the worst. She handled the Desert Technologies industrial espionage case last year," Alex said, remembering her grandfather mentioning it. "That cost the company incredible amounts in fines. Essentially put them out of business."

"And I'm sure there have been more," Tory added.

"I'll look into that aspect," Kayla said. "I've

got some contacts in Tucson. I just need someplace to start."

"Maybe Sam can do a little hacking on the side, come up with some names for you," Alex suggested, knowing there wasn't a system in the world that CIA operative Samantha St. John couldn't eventually crack. "If we can get a message to her."

No one said anything else for a few moments, but Alex could almost feel this wondrous set of brains working, and felt a brief flash of pride amidst the pain, to belong to such a group of women. She would tell them all how thankful she was that they'd seen through her protective reserve to the real Alex inside, and made her one of them. As soon as this was over, she was going to suggest they all get together and renew the Cassandra promise to each other.

"There's another thing," Kayla said finally.

"What?" Tory asked. Alex could almost see her reporter's mind working; investigating had always been Tory's favorite part of her work. She'd made her name famous by digging up the sometimes startling truths behind stories others took at face value.

"When I went to start searching some files at Athena after Alex left, looking for any clue to what's going on," Kayla said, "I...blacked out."

Alex's head snapped up. The others went suddenly tense, as well.

"You what?" she asked, her voice deceptively gentle.

"I passed right out. One minute I was fine, then

everything sort of faded away. I woke up on a cot in the infirmary." She glanced around, as if to be sure no one was within earshot. "I wasn't going to even mention it, except that it was so weird, the way it happened."

"We need everything," Tory said briskly. "Especially if it's weird."

"Yes," Alex agreed. Then, after a second's hesitation, asked, "Are you all right now?"

The faintest of smiles touched the corners of her mouth before Kayla nodded, as if she were glad Alex had been the one to ask.

"I'm fine. And I felt fine right up until I apparently went down. I didn't even get dizzy, nothing. It's never happened to me before, and hasn't happened since." She grimaced. "Betsy couldn't find anything wrong, and believe me, she poked and prodded everywhere. Of course, if she's involved, maybe she wouldn't have told me if she had found anything. But Christine was there, too, when I woke up."

"So," Tory said after a moment, "Rainy falling asleep at the wheel is definitely bull."

"Even if it were true, she should be alive," Kayla said. "I went to the crash scene, talked to the rescue guys and checked out her car." She glanced at the others before continuing. "Her seat belt failed."

"What?" Tory and Darcy exclaimed. Alex had already heard this bit of news.

"The mechanism apparently failed. If it had been working properly, the medics said she likely would have survived the crash."

There was silence again. Alex guessed each of them was feeling much the same thing. Anger. Loss. Suspicion. And at last it was Alex who put words to what they were all thinking.

"And what are the chances," Alex said softly, "that Kayla simply passed out, that Rainy fell asleep, and her seat belt failed?"

"Nil to none," Tory said.

"My sentiments exactly," Kayla said.

"Once is happenstance," Darcy said quietly.

"Twice is coincidence," Tory said.

Alex repeated the third line of the old axiom in tandem. "Third time is enemy action."

"But who is the enemy?" Kayla asked.

"I don't know," Alex said.

"But we'll find out," Tory said, in the voice of someone making a solemn vow.

"Yes," Darcy said with a spark of her old vigor, "we will."

Chapter 12

"In Rainy's files," Alex asked Kayla, "did you come across the name of Rainy's personal doctor?" They had just dropped Tory, Darcy and her son off at the airport for their respective trips home after an emotional gathering at the house where Marshall Carrington now lived alone. Christine was still there, waiting for a ride back to Athena Academy.

"Yes," Kayla said. "Dr. Halburg. Deborah, I think. I've got the address and number written down if you want it."

"Good. Thanks. Yes, I think I'll go and have a talk with her before I leave Tucson."

It was after four, but she might catch the doctor.

Kayla nodded. "I can take Christine home." She glanced over at Alex as they waited for the signal to change so they could exit the airport terminal area. "Do you think there's anything to what Shannon asked? That bit about medical experiments?"

Alex suppressed a shudder; that memory had crossed her mind more than once since the confrontation, and given her misgivings about her own appendectomy, had struck home in a very personal way.

"I don't know. It's a frightening thought. But that was a very specific question, and I have to wonder where she got the idea from in the first place. And the idea that we suspect the crash might not have been an accident."

"Especially since we're the only ones who knew," Kayla said.

"I know. And you and I have been careful not to talk on a cell connection that could be picked up."

Kayla nodded as she tapped a finger restlessly on the steering wheel. "I even called Tory at home the night she got back, rather than trying to call her cell while she was in Britain."

"And you know none of us has said anything to anyone outside Athena."

"But still she comes up with those particular questions. It's another suspicious thing to add to a stack that's already too big."

"It's getting messier and messier all the time," Alex agreed. "But we've got to get to the bottom of it."

"Are you going to be able to stay away from work much longer?" Kayla asked.

"I've still got a bit more personal leave time coming," she said. "My boss has been a bit of a pain about it, but since I've never taken any personal leave until now, he's stayed fairly calm. He's not happy about me taking it all at once, but there's not a whole lot he can do."

"Stick you on graveyard and make you file?" Kayla suggested wryly.

"He hasn't tried that yet," Alex said. "Is that the voice of experience speaking?"

"Yep."

"Who'd you tick off?"

"Which time?" Kayla asked.

Alex's mouth curved slightly. "That often, huh? How did you do that? Besides being female, Navajo and smart, I mean."

"That isn't enough?"

They both smiled then, relaxed and easy, and it was almost like old times between them. And it felt good, Alex admitted. Darned good.

The signal finally changed to green and Kayla moved the SUV smoothly into traffic. Once she was settled in a lane, she spoke again.

"What does your fiancé think about you taking off across the country like this?"

"He's not happy, but he understands. Or if he doesn't, he doesn't say so."

"Wise man."

"It's more that nothing rattles him much."

"I imagine to be a heart surgeon like he is, you have to be steady."

Someone had clearly been keeping Kayla up-to-date if she not only knew Alex was engaged, but that he was a doctor. And a heart surgeon specifically. She wondered if the information had been offered, or if Kayla had asked about her.

"He's that, all right. Unshakable. Although sometimes stick-in-the-mud fits better."

She hadn't meant to say that, but that kind of thing had been popping out lately. All of her small dissatisfactions seemed to be bubbling to the surface, manifesting in stray thoughts and slips of the tongue like this one. She'd chalk it up to tension about Rainy, but if she was brutally honest she had to admit it had been happening even before.

Kayla changed lanes to dodge a truck that was spitting out rocks from its uncovered load. "Doesn't sound like you're very happy with him right now."

"He's a brilliant surgeon, and saves a lot of lives," Alex said, aware she was sounding a bit defensive. But what she was saying was true. "And he's generous, calm and very patient. He doesn't like my choice of work, particularly, but he understands how important it is to me. Just as I understand how important his is. It's a...comfortable relationship."

"Comfortable?"

"Yes," Alex said, not liking the sound of it herself when she said it out loud. "Emerson's all right."

"Emerson?" Kayla's voice rose just slightly, as did one arched eyebrow.

"Yes. It's a family name. The first one was named after the poet."

"But…do you really call him that?"

Alex frowned, puzzled. "It's his name. What else would I call him?"

"I don't know." Kayla shot her a sideways look. "I guess I just have a hard time imagining anyone calling out 'Emerson' in the middle of having sex."

Alex flushed. "That's not a problem, since we've decided to wait until we're married."

Kayla blinked. "Wait? Haven't you been engaged nearly a year?"

That the ease with which Emerson had suggested they wait until they were married and the fact that it had been his idea in the first place bothered her, was not something Alex often admitted. It wasn't like she was a virgin saving herself for marriage, after all. As time went on, she was beginning to worry about whether they were going to be compatible or not. And Kayla's astonishment rubbed along that particular nerve, which was already a bit raw.

"And your point would be?" she asked in her chilliest Forsythe voice.

"Nothing. Nothing at all." Kayla fell silent. Rather pointedly silent.

"If there's something you want to say, just say it," Alex said, although she wasn't sure they wouldn't be better off if she just let it pass. They'd been slowly heading toward mending the rift between them, and now the old monster seemed to be rising anew.

"There's nothing I have any business saying. I'm hardly in a position to dispense advice on the subject."

Caution warred with the need to get it all out, even though it might open up the barely scarred-over wound between them. Alex finally decided there was no point in healing if it just covered up an infection that still raged.

"What advice would that be?" she asked carefully. "That we shouldn't get married without having had sex? Or that there's something wrong with us?"

Kayla hesitated for a rather long moment. Alex waited. Kayla gave her a quick glance, then shrugged.

"At least when I made my big mistake," she said, "I did it with passion."

Alex bit back a snappy reply. She didn't want to go back to the nearly nonexistent relationship of before and the painful truth of what Kayla had said stopped her.

Passion.

Yes, if there was something missing in her personal life, it was passion. Emerson would find such strong emotion unseemly, she was sure. He liked his life calm, tidy and organized, and passion was not. Passion was high-strung and messy. Passion made you act first and think later, which was something she couldn't recall Emerson ever doing since she'd known him.

He was passionate about his work, she knew that. The hours he put in certainly suggested it. She had finally decided his style of passion was simply different than hers, not that it didn't exist.

Or perhaps he was so passionate about his work that there was none left for anything else.

Including her.

And suddenly she saw her whole relationship with Emerson Howland through new eyes, and she didn't like what she was looking at. And for the sake of restoring a friendship that had once been at the center of her life, the least she could do was admit it.

"Touché," she said quietly.

Clearly startled at the concession, Kayla glanced at her for a brief moment before she had to turn her attention back to the road.

"You're not angry?"

"Yes, I am angry. But not at you. At myself, for letting my life…slide. I'm going to have to do something about that. Soon."

"You will," Kayla said, sounding relieved. "You're the strongest woman I've ever known."

"Don't sell yourself short. You've done well," Alex said softly. "As Tory said, you pulled it out."

Kayla let out a slow, drawn-out breath, as if she'd been holding it for a very long time. "I admitted long ago that Mike was a mistake. But because of him, I have Jazz. And that makes up for it."

Alex almost told her then, almost poured out her fears that what had been done to Rainy had also been done to her. Her fears that she might never have her own child to hold and cherish. That she would never have what Kayla had. And the sudden, unexpected desire to have it was an irony not lost on Alex, considering Kayla's means of getting it had been what had driven the wedge between them.

But at the last second she held it all back. She could see no sense in confusing the issue when she wasn't certain it was even true.

But she made up her mind to find out, as soon as the opportunity arose. She needed to know. Had to know.

Even if she dreaded the answer.

Dr. Deborah Halburg's office was in a fashionable building with a wonderfully cool—relatively speaking, since the temperature was into triple digits today—underground parking garage. There were several cars already parked there, but the lot was by no means full. Alex drove past a Mercedes dwarfed by a big luxury SUV, then a long, black BMW, a nondescript dark blue sedan and a pearl-white Lincoln. Mostly very upscale, she thought as she found a spot in the middle of the row where the elevators were, at the far end of the garage.

The garage elevator opened into a glass-and-marble lobby graced with southwestern art ranging from a mural of a coyote howling at the desert moon to a Kokopelli statue that actually played flute music. While Alex loved the haunting sounds of the native American flute, she found it somewhat disconcerting here amid all the marble and glass. To her it was music for the canyons and the wild places.

She crossed the cool, elegant lobby to the bank of three elevators on the far wall. She pushed the button to summon a car, and while she was waiting for one to arrive she read the directory next to them to confirm she had the right suite number from Kayla.

The elevator doors opened with a quiet whoosh, and she stepped inside. The elegance continued here, with marble and mirror. She pushed the button for the seventh floor, and instinctively scanned the car as the doors closed and it began to rise. There was the standard trapdoor in the ceiling, and a smoked glass bubble in one corner that she guessed hid a surveillance camera.

The numbers of the floors were announced with a chime worthy of Westminster. When the light labeled seven lit up, the door slid open to reveal a foyer furnished like some grand hotel. A long table sat beneath a huge mirror on the opposite wall, and on the table sat a huge arrangement of flowers. Hibiscus, fragrant frangipani and a couple of others she didn't know the names of offhand, but a tropical luxury here in the desert she was sure. And they were real, there was no question about that.

Since she had grown up with this kind of elegance, she had a pretty good idea how much it cost.

Assuming there was an arrangement on every floor, and likely several more besides, replacing the flowers alone—for she was certain no droopy or fading blooms were ever allowed—would be nearly a full-time job.

The atmosphere of elegance and wealth made her think of her mother. And the thing she thought of was her mother's reaction when Alex had told her she preferred to do the gardening herself, to get her own hands dirty. Her mother had been appalled at the idea—although she preferred it to some of Alex's less genteel pursuits.

The rock climbing about put her over the edge, Alex thought. Funny how belting around a course with dozens of fences aboard over a half-ton of hot-blooded horse was acceptable, but a simple climb to the top of a rock face was not. Her mother lived by a strange set of rules, rules Alex had been forever breaking. That her brother had gotten away with so much more, simply because he was a boy, was a double standard she had bucked until the day she'd left her mother's home for good. Only the fact that Ben had agreed with her, and on occasion fought it beside her, had made it bearable even that long.

Shaking her head as if to clear it of useless reminiscing, she looked around. A polished brass plaque directed her to her left for suite numbers 701-705. Only five suites taking up an entire side of this building gave her a clue as to the spaciousness of the offices. Rainy had paid a high price,

Alex guessed, in her effort to conceive a child. It made what had possibly happened to her even more infuriating.

The door to Dr. Halburg's office stood ajar by a fraction of an inch. Alex almost laughed at herself as she stared at it for a moment, memories flooding her. This was the third door she'd found ajar since this chaos had started, and each time she'd found somebody with no business there behind them. But this was a doctor's office, in a large office building, surely...

Making assumptions had gotten her into trouble twice already. This time she'd be ready for anything, and when she opened the door to find a receptionist busy behind a counter and patients sitting quietly in the waiting room, she'd feel relieved, not foolish.

She shifted her shoulder bag and slid her fingers between the two sections so that she could retrieve her weapon in an instant. Then she nudged open the door.

The office was dark.

It was as elegantly, albeit somewhat more contemporarily, furnished as the rest of the building. But it was empty, except for some fish in a large, colorful saltwater tank. No patients. No receptionist. No lights on except one in the fish tank. And apparently, no doctor.

But the door had been open.

Silently, Alex stepped over to the high counter that enclosed the reception desk. Between the open door to the corridor and the fish tank, there was enough light for her to see even though there were no exterior windows. There were no files out on the desk, nothing to indicate anyone had been here at all today.

Curious, she walked around the counter and sat down in front of the computer. She assumed the appointment files would be secured by a password, but she thought it worth a try. And it was. She couldn't get into the appointment program, or any patient files, but she did manage to open up a calendar. A calendar that had an entry for two days ago, to notify all scheduled patients their appointments for the next ten days were cancelled and would be rescheduled later.

She frowned at the screen. Was the doctor herself ill? Family emergency? Her absence had obviously been last minute.

She sat for a moment longer, looking around. There was no sign of a file cabinet of any size, no patient records. She wondered if Dr. Halburg kept them in a separate room, or perhaps her personal office. There were many other types of businesses besides doctors in this building, she'd noticed, so she hoped they wouldn't be tucked away in a central file repository as was often the custom in hospitals or all-medical buildings.

She got up and headed through the door at the back of the reception area. Immediately she noticed one door of several, the one at the very end of the hall, was ajar.

Four open doors, she thought. What are the chances?

As Tory had said, nil to none. First, she looked around until she saw a door just to the left marked exit, which she guessed would put patients back out in the hall without having to trek back through the waiting room. Now that she had her escape route should she need it, she reached for her bag again, this time curling her fingers around the butt of her Smith & Wesson.

She crept down to the slightly open door. There must be an exterior window in this office, because light streamed through the crack. She listened for a moment, heard the faint rustle of paper.

The doctor?

She didn't think so. Her gut didn't think so.

She nudged the door with her toe, leaving both hands free.

She had barely three seconds to register the scene before her. A man silhouetted by the sunlight coming through the window across the room, bent over the large, cherrywood desk in the center of the office. Files scattered all over the gleaming surface.

The gun in his right hand.

She knew she hadn't made a sound, but he somehow seemed to sense she was there. The gun in his hand leveled on her as he turned.

She made a split-second decision and dived out of the doorway. She hadn't really expected him to shoot, and he didn't. But she'd had about enough of this. She'd had about enough of him.

She ran out the exit door she'd noted earlier and, guessing he would come after her, she headed not for the elevators but for the stairwell at the end of the hall. She would have hit the button for the elevator as a false trail, but she doubted she'd have had time. She knew in seconds that she was right; she barely got through the door to the stairwell—holding it so it closed quietly—before he raced out into the hallway.

The stairway was much more utilitarian than the rest of the building, although it was still painted in coordinating colors rather than the usual institutional gray or white. It was also carpeted.

That would help, she thought. Figuring he would see the stairway and check it out, she grabbed the railing and went over, dropping down to the next floor landing. The carpet indeed muffled any sound.

One more floor, she thought, in case he's thorough.

She went over the railing of the landing again, down to the fifth floor landing. She'd noticed on the floor above that there were round metal cross supports beneath the stairs. With a leap, she was able to grab one. She doubled up, hooking her feet over another support and lifting her body upward. Now she should be out of sight even if he came down to the next landing and peered over. She could have gone through the door onto another floor, but she didn't want to risk the noise, plus, she didn't want a second closed door between them. She wanted to be able to hear what he did.

She'd barely gotten herself into position when a door above her opened. It sounded the right distance away to be the seventh floor door she'd gone through. She waited, listening. Nothing happened for a moment. Was he listening as she was? Then steps began, down the flight above her, to the first landing she'd jumped to.

Okay, so he was thorough.

Assuming it was him. For the first time she wondered what she would say if a startled stranger saw her. But on the next landing, the one above her, the steps stopped again. She held her breath. He was so close now she swore she could smell him, swore she got the faintest whiff of some spicy kind of aftershave or something.

What a stupid thing to notice while you're hanging here like a giant redheaded bat, she snapped at herself. Keep on task here, Alexandra!

The only time she called herself that was when she was angry at herself. And she was now, because her mind was wandering when she should be focused on evading the man hunting for her.

She closed her eyes, hung there and listened.

Steps again. Retreating this time. And at last the upper door opening and closing again. And then, fainter, another door. He'd gone back to the office.

Still she waited, in case it had been a feint. But at long last she let herself down, gratefully; clinging to those supports for that long had taken some strength out of her. She shook her arms a little, letting the muscles relax after the exertion.

And then she reached for her cell phone and called the cops.

Let Mr. FBI Special Agent Justin Cohen wiggle his way out of this one.

Alex felt a great sense of satisfaction as she sat in her rental car a block away and saw two Tucson Police units arrive. She'd been careful to make her anonymous report casual, saying she'd just passed the office door, seen it open and heard something inside, when she knew the doctor was gone.

She hadn't mentioned the gun; for all her irritation she didn't want the guy to get shot by cops going in thinking they had an armed burglar on their hands. At least, not until she learned if he had something to do with Rainy's death. And he would get it all straightened out, she was sure; for all their irritation with the feds, as Kayla had mentioned, locals still had respect for that FBI badge. But with any luck, it would take him a while to worm his way out of it, explain why he had broken into a well-known doctor's office.

If he'd fired that shot, then he *would* be in trouble. She'd have seen to that. No federal agent took being shot at lightly.

But he hadn't. He'd been under control. All that FBI training.

First she'd caught him in the infirmary at Athena. Then he turned up at Rainy's funeral. And now she'd found him breaking into Rainy's doctor's office. What on earth was going on? What was he really after? He'd been going through files, it seemed....

The scene played back in her head again, that instant when he'd seemed to sense her presence and begun to turn. She'd recognized him as Justin Cohen immediately, even though he'd been only a silhouette against the window.

Her breath caught.

Perhaps because he'd been a silhouette.

The amorphous memory that had been skating around the edges of her mind since the encounter with him at Athena suddenly settled, and began to take shape. She sat there, slightly stunned, thinking of a boy she'd caught a glimpse of so many years ago. A boy they'd all built adolescent fantasies and dreams around, giggling into the night.

Could Justin Cohen be the Dark Angel?

Chapter 13

The Dark Angel.

The mysterious legend of Athena.

The memories and stories played in her mind as she made the drive back to Athena Academy.

It had begun as most legends did, with a kernel of truth, that being the first time he'd been found trespassing on the Athena grounds as a boy, making his wild accusations. It was then embroidered upon by successive classes of impressionable young students, each one adding their own layer to the story whispered in darkened dorm rooms, until the midnight intruder had become an almost mythic figure.

Alex was sure the process had continued long

after she had left Athena, and wondered where it stood today, if the Dark Angel had grown even further into fabled fame. Who knew what actions and motives had been ascribed to him by the students by now? He could be the modern Arizona version of Robin Hood by this time. Maybe he had superpowers.

If she hadn't herself been one of the few to ever actually see him, she probably would have doubted his existence. And as she had told Christine, the fact that she had seen him really had increased her cachet at Athena. Girls would cluster around, begging her to tell the story one more time. New girls would be sent to her for the introduction to the legend. For the first time in her life she had understood what cronies of her grandfather meant when they talked about someone dining out on a story.

So she had known he existed then, and she was almost certain she had seen him again just an hour ago. Then he had been a wild, shatteringly beautiful boy just out of his teens, afire with the passion of his certainty that somehow Athena was responsible for his sister's death.

Now she guessed he was in his mid-thirties. And he was still darkly striking, but with the mature handsomeness of a man, not the youthful beauty of a boy. His face was fully adult now, his features strong, his body filled out from that near-skinny teenage gangliness. She hadn't been close enough to see his eyes all those years ago. Now she knew they were an amazing blue-green, burning with bright, fierce passion. The students had never been told his name, but Alex was certain Christine Evans would confirm it.

When she'd seen the Angel, he'd been about twenty. And to her somewhat naive, teenage eyes, he'd seemed the most romantic, exciting male creature alive.

But if she was remembering correctly, the first time he'd broken into Athena had been five years before that, the year after Rainy had started at the academy. She could summon up only the sketchiest of details of that time, since the staff had been so careful not to speak of him or his actions in front of students. She knew only that his sister had died and he had somehow become convinced Athena Academy was, if not totally responsible, at least involved in whatever had happened to her. Alex never really understood why, or even how she had died, because that had also been among the things the adults didn't discuss in front of them.

Which of course had only made the legend grow larger and faster.

Her cell phone rang as she was pulling in front of the guest bungalow, the special ring that signaled it was one of the Cassandras. She parked and went for it immediately, sliding it out of the belt clip and glancing at the screen. Kayla. She hit the talk button.

"Alex here."

"It's me. I'm heading for a dead zone so I've only got a minute. I've been looking into that other possibility we were discussing."

Alex knew she meant what Tory had brought up, the chance that this had nothing at all to do with Athena. She didn't think any of them really believed it, but Tory was right, it was possible, and had to be pursued.

"And?"

"So far nothing, at least with the people you mentioned. All scattered, and as far as I can tell, none even in the state any longer."

"But there are others?"

"Yes. Sam came through for us via e-mail. She gave me a name. Someone who's a guest in one of our state-sponsored hotels, with lots of contacts and reasons to be angry. I'm headed there now."

So, because of Rainy, somebody was in an Arizona state prison. That would be reason enough to want revenge, certainly. "Anything I can do?"

"Not at the moment, thanks. Just wanted somebody to know where I was going and why."

Alex heard what she wasn't saying, that none of the Cassandras could take any chances, not now.

"Good thinking," she said.

"I'll check back with you tonight. Later," Kayla said, and as if cued by her words the call was dropped.

Alex disconnected on her end, and found herself feeling good about the fact that Kayla had chosen her to call. Of course, she could have been the only one reachable at the moment; but Alex decided to accept her first thought and not second-guess.

Since the cell phone connection had been short-lived, she hadn't been able to tell Kayla what she suspected about Justin. And probably wouldn't have, not on the cell, not until they knew for sure what connection he had to everything.

But still, she wondered what Kayla's reaction would have been. She supposed it would depend on what the answers were to the questions Alex had been wrestling with when Kayla had called with her news. Tough questions she had no answers for. Yet. Like why was he back at Athena now, all these years later? Could he still be carrying that grudge, the cause imagined or not? The idea intrigued her. Could anybody really love a sibling that much, to pursue this madness for two decades?

She tried to imagine if something happened to Ben. She'd be heartbroken, of course. No matter how he annoyed her with his seemingly aimless lifestyle, he was her brother, they had a lifetime of memories together and she loved him. If something happened to him, if he died and if there was something suspicious about his death, would she have the resolve to hang on that long?

The answer came to her in a different form, when she thought about simply walking away now from whatever had happened to Rainy, who was not even a blood relation to her. The moment she did, the answer became as clear as the desert sky.

Oh, yes, she had the resolve.

So she had to believe the Dark Angel would as well. Justin Cohen, she corrected herself. Now that she knew his name, it would be better to use it. Take some of the mystique away, so she could think about him more rationally.

But that still left the question of exactly what he was after. The simple answer would be that he wanted the truth about what happened to his sister. But things that involved love and family and death were rarely simple. Alex knew that as well as anyone who worked in the law enforcement field. So even if he was looking for answers, if and when he found them, what then? What did he plan to do with whatever he discovered, if there was even anything to discover? Was he looking for retribution? Revenge, perhaps on any Athenan he could get his hands on?

Had he already gotten his hands on one of them, and had she died in a freak one-car accident as a result?

Alex sat there for a very long time, heedless of the heat, her thoughts tumbling. Everything that had happened since Rainy had called her, asking her to come to Athena, no questions asked, ran through her mind. Just the fact that Rainy had invoked the Cassandra promise put this out of the realm of the ordinary.

She supposed it was possible Justin Cohen wasn't an enemy, but her instincts were so thoroughly aroused right now everything seemed suspicious to her. And his actions definitely fell into that category. Yet, somehow, realizing he was that boy who had so desperately wanted the answers to his sister's death changed her feelings a little. It was as if they were on the same kind of crusade, and for the first time she truly understood what had driven him all these years.

She wondered if her trick of calling the police on him had gotten him into trouble at the field office in Phoenix. And it suddenly struck her, the unexpectedness of the Dark Angel having become an FBI agent. Why? Had he been driven to that course by his obsession with his sister's death? Had he had some idea he could one day use his position as an agent to open doors closed to him back then?

She thought back to her own academy days, the hardest sixteen weeks of her life. She'd been in good shape, or so she'd thought, but the physical demands had been beyond what she'd imagined. And the mental demands were only tempered by the fact she'd had the unique training offered at Athena.

So, would someone really go through the entire, difficult process of becoming a special agent—and with a record of getting in trouble, even if Athena hadn't prosecuted him for burglary as they could have, it had to have been more difficult for him than for the average guy—just to risk it all for a years-old fixation?

And the bottom line was still, why now? Why had he come back now, of all times?

Suddenly all the thoughts, questions, and puzzles whirling in her mind were too much, and she leaped out of the car. Swiftly she walked inside to the phone.

She picked up the receiver and dialed the extension that would ring in Christine's bungalow. When the woman answered, she wasted no time on preliminaries.

"Did the Dark Angel have any connection to Rainy?"

"What?" Christine asked, clearly startled.

"When he was caught here the first time, when Rainy was a second year, was there a connection?"

"Not that I'm aware of," Christine said. "Why on earth do you ask?"

"Because he's here again."

"What?" Christine repeated, clearly startled again. "The Dark Angel? You're not serious?"

"Justin Cohen," Alex said, knowing that the name would make her point, since none of the students were supposed to know it.

"Why, yes, that was his name. How did you find out? We tried very hard to keep all that…hysteria away from you girls."

"You succeeded. We never knew his name."

"But you know it now," Christine said slowly.

"Yes. Remember that FBI agent I caught snooping around in the infirmary?"

"Yes."

She waited, silently, for Christine to make the connection. It didn't take long.

"I…you mean he is Justin Cohen? The Dark Angel? Are you certain?"

"I ID'd him through the FBI. But you would be certain, too, if you'd actually seen him. He was at the graveside service. And I saw him again at Rainy's doctor's office. He was apparently searching through her files."

"The FBI is investigating this?" Christine sounded both astonished and upset.

"No."

"Then what was he—"

"He's apparently doing this on his own, from what I can find out."

"Oh." Christine went very quiet for a moment. "You mean he's still on his crusade?"

"So it would seem."

"But…you think he was looking for Lorraine's files, at her personal physician's office? Whatever would he want them for? What does that have to do with his sister?"

"My question exactly."

"I see. No, Alex, honestly, there was no connection between them that I know of." She paused a moment before adding, "But it does seem very odd that he should turn up just now, doesn't it?"

"Very odd," Alex agreed, although the word she would have used was suspicious. Very suspicious.

"What are you going to do?"

Somehow, during this discussion, the chaotic thoughts had calmed slightly, and out of the mess had crystallized the only logical course of action.

"I'm going to find him," she said. "And ask him what the hell he's up to."

"Hopefully he'll tell you, you being a fellow FBI agent," Christine said.

"Oh, he'll tell me," Alex promised her.

One way or another, he'll tell me.

She realized she was pacing, already eager to start, take some action. Any action. Mental puzzles were all well and good, but sometimes she just needed to do something.

But before she hung up, one last question to Christine popped out before she even thought about it.

"How did his sister die?"

There was a long pause that made the answer all the more significant when it finally came.

"She died in childbirth."

Alex's pacing came to an abrupt halt. Christine said no more, but long after she'd hung up Alex still stood there, her gaze unfocused, all those thoughts, possibilities, improbabilities and coincidences rattling around in her head all over again.

Childbirth.

Rainy's eggs.

What in the hell was going on?

Chapter 14

Alex had spent a restless night and woken determined to take action. Christine had her hands full with all the new students this week. Kayla had work. Alex's job was to pin down the Dark Angel. But where?

She had to think of him as Justin, she stopped and corrected herself yet again. If she ever let that out he'd probably never talk to her, since he likely had no idea he'd become such a famous figure at Athena, let alone one with a nickname like that.

Through Kayla she found out that Justin had talked his way out of the situation she'd tossed him into with the police. Alex sat in her car for a moment, thinking.

She'd done nothing so far this morning but dress in the lightest-weight clothing she'd brought and then run down to her car, when she should have been figuring all this out. Lot of good it did her to be sitting here in the car—other than to put the air-conditioning on full blast so she could stand to be in it—with no idea of where she was going to go first.

Mental abilities had been stressed as much as and sometimes more than the physical at Athena. And that had included understanding people. Her time with the FBI had only honed that ability. She just had to remember that although this was so very much more personal, she still needed to handle it as if it were a case she'd been assigned to.

So, *think!* she ordered herself silently.

What would Justin do now? She ticked off the possibilities.

The first one that came to her was that he could go back to Dr. Halburg's office. Now that would fit the determination—or the stubbornness—of the man, or at least what she knew of him. Anyone who could hang on to a grudge for twenty years wouldn't give up at the first sign of trouble.

She also had a sneaking suspicion it was what she herself would do, under the circumstances.

She supposed he could quietly go home, wherever that might be. Somewhere in Phoenix or a suburb, most likely. But that course of action didn't seem very likely to her. This was a man with a mission, and going tamely home to sulk wouldn't get it done.

He could continue his search somewhere other than the doctor's office. Back at Athena, perhaps. She considered that for a moment, then reached for her cell phone and called Christine, who was currently in her office in the administration building.

"That subject we were speaking of yesterday?" she said. "That…returning pest?"

"The winged one?" Christine asked, quick to pick up both on her meaning and the need for discretion.

"Yes, that's the one," Alex said. "Keep an eye out. It may come back."

"Oh? Do you think it will be flitting around the same light?"

"Probably. If it does show up again, catch it and hold it. I want to see exactly what it is."

"I think I can manage that," Christine said.

I have no doubt, Alex thought. And, she added as she hung up, good luck to anyone who thinks you can't because you're a bit gray.

"Now, back to the possibilities," she muttered as she stood the phone in the cup holder of the rental car.

If he didn't go home, to the scene of the most recent crime, or to Athena, then where would he go?

Maybe back to Phoenix and the FBI office, to try and cover his butt there should anyone from Tucson P.D. decide to make a call and let his superiors know what he was up to. Now that was a definite possibility. In fact, he might just try that first, then go on to one of the other options. Although she didn't know what kind of story he could concoct that would explain what he was doing in a closed doctor's office without betraying what she assumed he was keeping secret from his employer.

Maybe he's so far gone he doesn't care about that anymore, she thought. Maybe he's just decided to go for broke, damn the torpedoes, throw caution to the winds, and all those other clichés men use when they wanted to justify an action they had to know was reckless.

As her own thoughts echoed in her mind, she suddenly found herself trying to picture Emerson doing anything reckless. She couldn't imagine any circumstances under which that would happen. And for the first time she wondered if any of his great success as a surgeon resulted from playing it safe, from simply refusing to do operations that were too chancy.

Deciding that was unfair, and that she didn't know anywhere near enough about his work to make that kind of judgment, Alex turned her attention back to the problem at hand. Finding Justin Cohen.

Christine would handle it if he showed up back at Athena, so that was covered. She really didn't think he'd go and sit quietly at home; if he was that type, he wouldn't have shown up at Athena or Rainy's funeral in the first place.

That left the FBI office and Dr. Halburg's.

"Okay, then," she murmured aloud, "I have to drive through the outskirts of Phoenix to get to Tucson anyway, I'll just go by way of the FBI office."

It was only two or three miles off I-10, if she was remembering correctly. And she thought she was; while still at Athena she'd spent some time there observing.

She put the now blissfully cool car in gear and headed off the Athena grounds and toward the freeway. She took the eastbound ramp and brought the car quickly up to the speed limit. She settled in for the drive; it was fifty miles to the 7th Street ramp, so she had some time. She wasn't quite sure what she was going to do when she got there…. It struck her then, the obvious answer.

"Well, duh," she muttered.

She started checking off-ramps the moment she got into the urban sprawl that was now Phoenix. She looked at the signs of business that looked easily accessible, spotted a 24/7 convenience store and bailed off the freeway. She pulled up to the pay phone in front, wondering if soon anyone but people who had something to hide would ever use them.

She checked the phone book, then dug out a quarter. She picked up the receiver then immediately dropped it, it was so hot. She really was out of the habits she'd learned here to deal with the heat.

She stepped back to the car and grabbed the linen jacket she hadn't put on because of the soaring temperature. She draped it over her hand and then picked up the receiver again. She took the quarter, slipped it into the slot and dialed.

"FBI," a deep male voice answered on the second ring.

"Yes, is Agent Cohen in?"

"I'll check. What's it regarding, please?"

She'd known that was coming. "I have some information he wanted, about some property I had stolen."

She hoped that would be enough, that the man who answered the phone would assume it was the receiving stolen property case and leave it at that. To her relief, he did.

"Hang on just a moment, please."

If she'd been smart, Alex thought, she'd have found a pay phone inside. Inside someplace air-conditioned. It was true that most times ninety-five degrees here didn't seem as hot as ninety-five in more humid D.C., but once it broke one hundred, it didn't matter much anymore.

As if on the thought she spotted a thermometer hanging outside a bank building. It read one hundred and nine. And as she watched, it rolled up to an even one hundred and ten. She stifled a groan and hoped the coolant system in her rental was in good shape, that the—

"I'm sorry, but Special Agent Cohen is in the field."

"Do you know when he'll be back?"

"I'd guess not until tomorrow. I'll be glad to take the information for him or have him call you."

"No, I'll call back tomorrow. Thank you," she said, hanging up quickly before he could protest or insist—or ask her what her name was.

She got back into the car and started the engine

so she could turn the air back on. For a moment she sat there and pondered, wondering if he were really gone or just not taking calls at the moment. But her gut was saying that her first guess had been the right one, that he would go back to Dr. Halburg's. Probably after business hours. She got back on the freeway and settled in for the two hour drive down to Tucson.

After a few miles with her mind racing in too many directions at once, she resorted to a time-tested tactic. She turned on the radio. It was tuned, loudly, to a station that made her wince, and she quickly hit a button. That put her on some classical music, which she left on. She didn't know enough about it to know this piece by ear, but she knew that classical sometimes worked best when she had a lot to think about. She guessed it was the lack of lyrics to distract her. Whatever problem she was facing got pushed just far enough back for her subconscious to work on.

But this time, when she reached Tucson she wasn't any closer to figuring this all out. There was no scenario she could come up with that fit all the scattered pieces they had that didn't also stretch her ability to suspend disbelief to beyond the breaking point.

It was easier, she thought, for those on the outside to believe in huge conspiracies. Those in the agencies that investigated such things knew how rare they really were, which was why they were so much harder to convince.

She was too early for the end of the day, so she stopped by the Carrington house and paid her respects again to Marshall, and to Rainy's parents, who were staying through the weekend.

She reached Dr. Halburg's office building hours later, more determined than ever to find the man who might have answers about Rainy's senseless death. At this hour, as the business day ended, the parking garage was emptier, and she saw as she went down the ramp that she would have almost her pick of spaces. She parked much closer to the elevators this time. She got out and turned to lock the rental's door. And froze midmovement.

She turned to stare down the row of parking spaces. She took three steps out into the lane and looked closer. She was sure of it, it was the same car. That same nondescript dark blue sedan she'd seen here before, between the Mercedes and the BMW. Nondescript enough to be a government car.

Only now it was parked in a different spot. All the way back near the entrance, which was why she'd missed seeing it until now. Backed in, in fact, as if someone were already feeling eager to leave.

Or escape.

She leaned back into the rental car to punch the trunk release and grab her linen jacket. She walked back to the trunk and opened it. She tossed in her bag, but before she locked it away, she took out the Smith & Wesson model 386 she favored not only because it held seven rounds instead of five, but because it could fire both a .357 magnum or the nearly universally available .38 special ammo. She slid it into a small clip holster, fastened the weapon at the small of her back and slipped on the linen jacket to cover it. She locked the trunk and the car, then slipped the keys into her pocket to free her hands completely.

She was glad now she'd worn lightweight, flexible canvas shoes. Contrary to the scenes on television or in movies that made her laugh and wince equally, running in high heels was never wise, not when one wrong step could result in a broken ankle for you and an escaped quarry for the Bureau.

Or in this case, an escaped quarry for herself.

Which makes me, she thought, as she took the same path she had this morning, just like him, in a way.

Maybe, she amended silently. She wasn't out for revenge, or retribution, just answers. Of course, she couldn't promise that when she got those answers her quest wouldn't change.

She retraced her route of yesterday. As she entered the cool marble lobby, she wondered how many times Rainy had walked this same path, perhaps praying for good news as she went, hoping against hope that this time there would be new life growing within her.

Alex's stomach tightened, and she fought off a shiver as her dear friend suddenly seemed so very close. It only pointed out to her how far away Rainy was in reality, and the shiver eventually won out. She picked up her pace.

She crossed the lobby at a trot. She spotted an office labeled Information just down the hallway. She decided to risk taking a moment or two to see if they knew anything about Dr. Halburg's absence.

The woman behind the desk was a friendly, grandmotherly type. Fortunately, she seemed to be the type to mind everyone else's business, as well. And was more than happy to share what she knew, even though she'd been about to leave for the day.

"Oh, yes, Dr. Halburg is on vacation. Well-earned, may I say. She works far too hard. She's an excellent doctor, the best in the city in her field, so she's very much in demand. But she needed this break, she was looking a bit weary. And I think this is the first vacation she's had since she moved into this building three years ago."

"Thank you," Alex said, escaping before the woman could start prying into her business there.

This time one of the elevators was already on its way down. She glanced around, wondering where she could hide if her quarry happened to be using this public exit.

There was a ladies' room just down the hall, and while she couldn't see the elevators, anyone who came out of them would have to walk through her field of vision. She ran quickly that way and ducked inside. She grabbed a paper towel and rapidly folded it into a small, thick square that she used to prop the door open a tiny fraction of an inch, just enough to press her eye to.

A well-dressed woman, elegant and imperious enough to fit the building, was the only person who came out. A woman who reminded Alex of her mother for more reasons than one. She waited a minute to be sure, then went back to the elevators.

The doors slid silently open when she reached the seventh floor. Alex peeked around from where she'd hidden in front of the control panel. The foyer was empty. She stepped out of the car. Knowing now where the exit door was, and its proximity to the doctor's office, she paused there. As she expected, she wasn't able to open it from the outside.

It suddenly occurred to her that there was another unlabeled door a bit farther down the hall from the patient exit, and she wondered if it could be a direct exit from Dr. Halburg's personal office. She closed her eyes for a moment, visualizing the layout of the suite as she recalled it. She'd only gotten a brief glimpse of the office yesterday, but as she reconstructed it in her mind, it seemed possible.

Best if she assumed it was, she decided. Assume he had two exits, which complicated things. Of course. She went down the hall.

This time the door to the office suite was closed. And locked. He was being more cautious this time. Assuming, of course, he was in there.

It took her about ninety seconds to do this lock. She was too rusty, she'd have to get in more practice. Then again, at the rate she was going she'd have plenty of practice before this was over.

This time she was the one who left the door open, so she could hopefully hear if he somehow got past her and went out the back way. She crept inside then stood and listened. She heard nothing, either in the reception area or back toward Dr. Halburg's office. She moved with exquisite care down the long hallway, pausing before the door to each examination room, listening, barely breathing herself before she risked a look inside, verified the room was empty, and went on to the next.

Finally she reached the doctor's office. The door was closed. She stopped to consider. There was no sign he was here this time, but she didn't think that meant much. He'd either been careless the first time, leaving those doors unfastened, or he'd done it intentionally in case he had to make a quick, silent exit. If it were her, she'd probably close the doors after herself, making the office appear untouched from the outside to any casual observer.

Which meant he could be anywhere. Behind any of these many doors, in any examination room or back in Dr. Halburg's private office. And if he was, testing the knob to see if it was locked could alert him and send him out that back door into the hall.

She leaned forward, pressing an ear to the tiny space between the door and the jamb and keeping her own breathing as quiet as she could. She heard nothing, no movement from inside.

Remembering the bright sunlight from the doctor's window, she glanced downward. Indeed, light spilled out from under the door. She knelt down and, knowing it was a bit risky, rested her head on the floor until she could peer under the door with one eye. She watched for movement. Nothing disrupted the flow of light, no shadow cut across it.

It was time. She'd done all she could from out here. It seemed the room was empty, but she had to work on the assumption an armed man, very likely with interests contrary to her own, was on the other side. So the only question left was whether to try to maintain secrecy for as long as possible, or go for the surprise—and noise—of speed.

Surprise, Alex thought. I'm tired of stealthing around.

She reached out and let her right hand hover just above the doorknob. Her fingers curled. She took a deep breath. Exhaled it until she was fully relaxed.

In one swift motion she grabbed, turned and pushed hard on the doorknob. It went easily. She dodged to one side, out of a possible line of fire. There was no reaction from inside, and she looked around through the opening door into what appeared to be an empty office.

She waited. No sound came, no movement.

She took one step inside.

An arm snaked out and grabbed her shoulder from behind. A voice, low and masculine, spoke.

"I've been waiting for you."

Chapter 15

Alex reacted instinctively and instantly. She spun around, breaking the grip on her shoulder before it could tighten. Face-to-face with her attacker, she moved her right knee. He reacted as quickly, pulling his hips back against an expected hit to the groin. The movement brought his chest slightly forward. Just as she'd hoped.

She grabbed his shoulders. Used his own forward motion to jam his chest downward. His position made it impossible for him to resist. She shot her knee upward, as hard as she could into the target he'd presented to her. Hit him just below the sternum.

Bull's-eye, she thought as she heard his breath

whoosh out. He doubled over. She gave a slight push backward. Felt his balance go. Released him and stepped back. Out of his reach. He hit the floor on his backside. Given the muscled shape of that backside, she didn't think he was hurt much.

She put one hand on the butt of the gun at the small of her back. She didn't pull the weapon on him, even though she was positive he was armed. Drawing on a fellow agent was more than she was willing to do.

Yet.

"Now," she said coldly, "you and I are going to have a little talk, Special Agent Cohen."

One arm still crossed tightly over his abdomen where she'd kneed him, he slowly looked up at her. She was more than a little pleased that it took him a moment to gather the wind to talk.

"Suckered me…didn't you?"

"Men," she said dismissively, "always think a woman's going to go for the groin."

His mouth twisted into a wry, pained smile, and he looked about to say something. Then she saw him notice the position of her right hand behind her back. The smile faded.

"That's not necessary," he said.

"Isn't it? You've become a chronic trespasser at Athena Academy, you show up at my friend's funeral, and then here, where you were obviously lying in wait and attacked me the moment I came in the door."

"I didn't attack you," he began.

"I'm a woman alone, you're a man," she pointed out. "What was I to think?"

His mouth twisted then, giving her a look she supposed she deserved. "Oh, please," he said. "Like you couldn't handle any guy that came along."

"How was I to know that you knew that? Besides, you're armed. But don't change the subject. What are you really doing, Special Agent Cohen?" She purposely used the full title again.

"Look, can I get up?"

He had the brains to ask, at least, she thought, and nodded.

"Well?" she prodded when he'd eased his way back onto his feet. The backside, she noted, was as fine as she'd remembered. And uninjured, apparently.

"I'm…on a case," he said finally.

Her fingers tightened on the grips of the pistol. "I doubt very much if you're going to find any leads on your stolen property case here in a doctor's office. A fertility doctor's office."

For an instant surprise glinted in his eyes. Likely at her knowing about his official case, she guessed. But to his credit, he didn't try to deny her words.

"Why do you think I just waited here for you to show up?"

"Good question," she snapped. "Why?"

"Because I've been trying to get you alone, so I could talk to you."

"You had a chance to talk to me back at Athena."

"Not before that…woman arrived."

He snorted inelegantly. Not that it detracted from those smoldering, dark good looks. If she'd had to imagine how the gorgeous boy she'd seen that night would have turned out, this would be it. He was standing straighter by now, and she could see he was well over six feet. And solid. Very solid. She realized how lucky she was to have landed that knee in the exact spot necessary to wind him.

"Look, I meant what I said. I wanted to talk to you. I figured you'd come back here, and—"

"I only came back here because I figured you would."

"Exactly."

Temper jabbed at her at the idea that she'd been so predictable to him. But then, he'd been predictable to her, as well.

"So, we both want answers," she said. "You go first."

His mouth quirked upward at one corner. For an instant he looked like the Dark Angel again, that intense, impassioned young man who had branded her consciousness by his very existence. He took her breath away now just as he had then, and when he spoke again, it took her a moment to tune in to the words.

"—both get what we want."

If he knew what she wanted, she thought in that

moment, they'd likely both be embarrassed beyond belief. She was, simply by thinking about it.

Snap out of it! she ordered herself sharply. "What do you mean?" she said, figuring that was safe enough.

"I mean, can we go somewhere and talk?"

She glanced around the office, but still kept him in her peripheral vision. "Don't you want to tidy your mess?" she asked sweetly.

"It's not my mess."

Her gaze snapped back to his face. "What?"

"It was like this when I got here the first time. Why do you think I had my gun out? I didn't know if whoever it was was still here."

Her gaze darted quickly around the room. The only thing out of place was the pile of tossed folders, apparently patient files, that covered the mahogany desk and spilled over onto the floor. Instinctively her mind shifted into crime-scene mode, and she found herself thinking it would take light fingerprint powder and dark cards to lift anything off the very dark wood of that desk.

As for the folders and papers, she'd be looking at DFO and then maybe ninhydrin, the reagents that reacted with the amino acids in the sweat that caused fingerprints to be left. She grimaced at the thought. The chemical was hazardous, irritated the eyes, skin, respiratory system, and since it meant using the fume hood, it was one of her least favorite processes.

And lifting prints without destroying any writing on the documents was tricky. Not that she would expect, considering these people seemed to be pros, to find any prints.

Except perhaps those of Special Agent Justin Cohen.

"And here I thought it was just for my benefit."

"If it was, it failed miserably, didn't it?"

"Meaning?"

"You're FBI, too."

She blinked. He'd obviously done some checking of his own.

"A buddy of mine in the office said somebody from D.C. had called, asking about me," he explained as if she had actually asked. "Tried to pass it off as a woman with a personal interest, but I haven't met a woman in years I haven't managed to piss off."

"Obsession will do that to a woman," she said easily.

"Obsession?"

"That's what this is all about, isn't it? You still have some crazy idea that someone at Athena is involved in your sister's death."

He seemed surprised at her knowledge. And this time she answered him as if he'd asked.

"You became rather a legend at Athena, after the first time you broke in. Everybody knew the story."

"Everybody," he said, as if through gritted teeth although his jaw didn't seem to clench, "knows nothing."

"Apparently you think you know something."

"I do. I always have."

"Funny, and here I thought the FBI beat fantasy out of its agents."

"It's not a fantasy. Look, I'll tell you the whole story. Then you decide."

She raised one brow. "And why am I any different than that 'everybody' who knows nothing?"

He hesitated. "I saw you that night. The second time I broke into Athena, seventeen years ago."

It was her turn to be surprised. She grimaced. "I was a kid then."

"Your hair hasn't changed much. When I saw you again it didn't take me long to connect you to the girl with that mass of red-gold hair."

"When?"

"What?"

"When did you see me this time? How long have you been watching us?"

"Since I read about the crash, and who the victim was, in the paper." He shrugged. "I'll tell you the whole thing, but we'd better get out of here. I'm not sure I can talk my way out of getting caught here again."

She hesitated just a moment longer, looking at him assessingly.

"Want me to give you my service weapon?" he asked, lifting one dark brown eyebrow.

"Not a bad idea," she said easily. "But I'll just keep mine handy."

"An armed truce, then?"

"Peace is best maintained between those evenly matched, someone once said."

"Lady, you've run me ragged since you got to Arizona, not to mention putting me on the floor just now," he said, his tone dry. "I'd say we were even, with or without sidearms."

She didn't miss the compliment, but chose not to respond. "What about whatever you were looking for here?"

"I told you, it was like this when I got here. These files are all *C*s. But," he added, "there's no file here for Lorraine Carrington."

It didn't surprise her, she'd expected something of the sort. She highly doubted this was just some filing that hadn't been done. Judging from Cohen's tone, he doubted it, too.

"I saw a coffee shop across the street," she said suddenly, not certain what had sparked the suggestion.

"That'll do, if we can find a quiet table away from everyone."

As it turned out that wasn't difficult; even iced-coffee drinks weren't selling briskly on this meltingly hot day. They left their cars in the cooler garage and walked across the street.

"I've gotten out of the desert heat habit," she muttered as the welcome blast of air-conditioned air hit her as they stepped inside.

"It's tough if you weren't born here."

She studied him as they sat down, him with a frappuccino and she with a lemonade iced tea.

"And you were?"

"Yes."

"And your sister?"

His fingers tightened around the plastic cup that held his chilled drink. "Let me tell you about her."

Alex opened her mouth to say she only wanted to know what his business was here and now, so she could decide if he was a threat to Athena, but just as quickly she closed it again. She did want to know what had driven the Dark Angel.

"All right," she said instead. It was what she'd come after him for, after all.

For a long moment he fiddled with the stir stick in his drink. "Crazy," he muttered. "I've thought about telling you this for days, but now I can't seem to figure out where to start."

"Tell me about your sister," she said quietly. "What was her name?"

"Kelly." He looked up at Alex then. "She was…incredible. Our parents were killed in a car crash when she was eighteen. I was only thirteen. They stuck me in foster care. But she worked like a dog, sometimes two jobs, trying to save enough money to convince the state she could take care of me."

"She must have loved you very much."

"She did. She was the only one who did."

"What happened?"

"She found a way to get enough money. More than enough. She didn't tell me that at first, though. She only told me she couldn't see me for a few months, but after that, we'd be back together for good."

"A few months? What did she have to do?"

He looked at her steadily, as if trying to calculate how she would react. Finally he said bluntly, "Be a surrogate mother."

Alex sucked in a harsh breath. Her mind began to race, and she had to rein it in.

"She took money for it, to help me, and it killed her."

"You mean…she died giving birth to someone else's child?"

"Yes."

A surrogate mother. Rainy's eggs. A shiver ran through her and she was glad when he began to speak again, because she couldn't think of a single thing to say.

"She saw it as a way to get the money she needed to get me out of foster care."

No wonder he was so obsessed with his sister, Alex thought. She'd essentially died for his sake.

"They paid her fifty thousand dollars," he said.

"That's a lot," Alex said neutrally. "And it was even more then."

He nodded, staring down at his cup as if the answer to life was floating by. When he didn't go on, Alex prodded slightly.

"Why couldn't she see you?"

His head came up. He looked at her intently. One corner of his mouth lifted in what could have been smile or grimace. "Bingo," he said softly.

"What?"

"That's what was fishy about the whole thing.

She said they couldn't know about me. That it was crucial they never find out I even existed."

"They?"

"The people who set it all up, and who would take care of her when the baby came."

Alex frowned. "What difference could it make if they knew she had a brother?"

"That's what I wanted to know. She couldn't tell me, she just said that they insisted she had to be single, with no ties."

Alex pondered that for a moment. "Maybe they just thought there would be less chance that she would change her mind and want the baby herself."

"That's what I thought, at first. But after she died…"

He stopped. He stared down at his drink. She looked at him, at the dark semicircles of thick lashes, in the unfair way of nature more beautiful than most women's.

"After she died," he went on, his voice low and taut, "I got to thinking that maybe they had wanted her not to have any ties for another reason. That maybe they just hadn't wanted her to have anyone who might come looking for her, or ask questions."

Disposable, Alex thought, the first word that popped into her mind.

She realized she'd become caught up in his story, and to be honest, a tiny bit fascinated with the idea of sitting here across from the Dark Angel as if it were normal. He was still every bit as intense and dramatically handsome as he'd been then, and after all those years of hearing the legend repeated it was difficult to believe he was really here.

A flash of heat shot through her, startling her. It was a moment before she realized that the attraction it had taken her a long time to admit to had morphed into something else, something hotter, stronger, deeper. She stared at him, the one part of her mind she could still call sane at this instant hoping fiercely he wouldn't look up and see her gaping at him like a landed fish.

What was happening? She was going to marry Emerson, she had no business going into heat over another man. Especially this one. She tried to quash the burgeoning feelings, told herself she was indulging in some adolescent fantasy gone amok, but she knew better. She'd been attracted to him before, yes, but it had only changed to this after she'd come to know him, admire him.

She knew then she was in big trouble. It was a tremendous effort for her to refocus on his story.

What he'd told her so far was so awful that it was with a great effort that Alex brought the conversation back to her main concern.

"What," she said, "does all this about your sister have to do with Athena?"

"I'm getting to that." He ran a finger through the condensation on the side of his plastic glass. "When the time came, Kelly called me from her apartment. Said the baby was coming, fast, and she'd be on her way to the hospital as soon as they came to get her. She sounded scared."

"They? Not medics or an ambulance?"

He gave her a sideways look. "No. Another fishy part of the deal." He paused, took a breath like a rider about to start a cross-country run, then plunged ahead. "The next day I hadn't heard from her. I called the hospital and they wouldn't tell me anything on the phone. So I went down there. Raised a ruckus, but they wouldn't let me see her."

Alex could picture it all too well. The young, desperate boy, helpless against an adult system that decided for him what he should know, where he should be, what he should do. It made her own gripes about her childhood and her mother seem pretty shallow and pointless. And that helped her wait quietly for him to continue when he could.

"Finally a doctor came, and he told me she and the baby hadn't made it. That there had been complications, bleeding…."

He stopped, and Alex stayed silent again; the memories were piling up on him, she could sense it, and knew this was not the time to prod him to hurry, even though she was impatient to find out what on earth all this had to do with Athena. Or at least, what it had to do with Athena in his mind.

Besides, she was feeling a bit of a pang herself, at the thought of a scared young girl, dying alone, in pain, surely feeling the whole world had turned against her when all she'd been trying to do was keep what was left of her little family together.

After a couple of moments he continued. "The hospital called the authorities, to take me back to the foster home."

"You just find out the only family you have died and they couldn't wait to turn you back over to foster care?" she asked softly.

He shrugged. "Oh, the nurses were really nice, and were worried about me, but what else could they do with an angry teen? Anyway, while I was sitting at the nurses' station—so they could keep an eye on me, I guess—before the child welfare people came to take me back, I heard them talking."

"The nurses?"

He nodded. "About the private nurse who had been taking care of her, and what a…a pain she was, ordering everybody to stay away from her patient."

Alex couldn't even begin to imagine what his feelings had been, a fifteen-year-old boy left alone in the world like that. No wonder he'd been looking for someone to blame, someone to hate. Life had not been kind to the young Justin Cohen. First his parents, then his sister. It really was amazing that he'd pulled himself together enough to end up where he was now. And perhaps not so amazing that she'd gotten all tangled up over him.

"And then, later, I found out about the fifty thousand in her bank account, which she'd instructed was to be mine if anything happened to her. Even after she was dead, she was still taking care of her little brother."

And suddenly Alex wished she hadn't called the cops on him yesterday. She didn't want him to lose what he'd managed to gain despite such a rocky start.

But there was still one question he hadn't answered.

"I understand, Justin," she said gently. "But I still don't know what all this has to do with Athena."

He looked up, met her gaze levelly. And answered. "That nurse I mentioned? The private one taking care of Kelly, and ordering everyone else to stay away from her?"

An idea leaped into her mind in the moment before he spoke and confirmed it.

"It was Betsy Stone."

Chapter 16

The cool air in the coffee shop, which had been so welcome when they'd come in, seemed icy cold to Alex now. It crept over her like the cold of the morgue. She rubbed at her bare arms, barely managing to suppress a shiver. She welcomed the distraction when her cell phone rang. She had planned to ignore it until she saw it was Kayla.

"Excuse me," she said, a mechanical expression of manners drilled into her from childhood.

Justin nodded, and she picked it up, wondering what Kayla would say if she mentioned who she was with right now, and what he had just told her.

"Nothing," Kayla said, before Alex could ask. "I saw the guy, and whatever kind of arrogant jerk he was before, the Arizona State Prison system has taken it out of him. A real reality check. He's just humbled enough that I believe him."

"Good enough for me. Can I call you later?" She would need to let Kayla know as soon as possible that she knew now who the Athena connection was.

"Sure. I'm heading back to the department."

"I'll reconnect with you there," she said.

After she'd hung up and set the phone down on the table, it took her a moment to bring herself back to the reality sitting across the table from her. Justin was looking at her as if he knew perfectly well that the call she'd just received had something to do with what they were sitting here talking about. But to his credit, he didn't demand that she tell him. He was apparently smart enough to realize she didn't trust him yet and wasn't about to tell him anything until and unless she did.

Instead he merely looked at her, a glint in his eyes she couldn't quite decipher, except that it held a hint of challenge.

"Afraid somebody might realize you're with me?"

She shoved her phone back into her purse with more force than necessary. "Hardly," she said, more vehemently than she'd wanted to.

He arched one dark brow at her. "Afraid of yourself with me, then?"

She just stopped her jaw from dropping. "Oh, please," she said. But behind the effort at sarcasm was a niggling doubt, and the fear that maybe he was right.

She forced herself to focus once more. She had no business wondering if she was falling for this man when there were far more important things for her to be concentrating on.

Betsy Stone, his dead sister's nurse. It all seemed so incredible, but really, was the story of Kelly Cohen's horrible death really any more unimaginable than Rainy's death was to them? Weren't the Athenans and this man dealing with the same kind of horrible nightmare, two decades apart?

"Go on," she said, her voice slightly hoarse from her tangled emotions.

After a moment Justin nodded and picked up his story. "I could never prove Athena had anything to do with what was done to Kelly or her death. But I knew Stone worked there. It was all I had to go on."

"You were only fifteen," Alex said, because she felt as if she needed to say something.

His mouth quirked. "Believe me, I know. I was never allowed to forget that fact. Nobody wanted to take me seriously. No one even wanted to talk to a kid about it, especially a wildly angry one."

Something in his tone got through her chill. She remembered the young man she'd seen that night, a few years after the first time he'd gone to Athena, could imagine how much angrier and fiercer he must have been the first time, immediately after his beloved sister, his only relative, had died.

"And a scared one?" she suggested softly.

"Oh, very," he admitted easily. And she liked him for that. Among other things, some of which she hadn't admitted even to herself. "I didn't know what was going to happen to me."

"Did they send you back to your foster home?"

He nodded. "It's not that they were that bad, my foster family, they really weren't. I've heard of much worse. But after all this had happened, they kept me on a pretty tight rein. They were ordered to, I think."

"I'm sure they were worried about you."

"About being responsible for what I did, anyway," he said. Then he shook his head as if at his own words. "No, that's not fair. They did the best they could, and they were genuinely trying to help."

And again she liked him for saying that. It would have been easy for him to have come to hate everyone associated with that time. That he didn't, or wouldn't let himself, said a lot about him. It seemed there was much to admire about him besides the looks that made her pulse kick into overdrive.

His words also told her he was more rational about it all than perhaps she would have liked. If he wasn't a crazed obsessive, then there was more likely some foundation to his story and he couldn't be dismissed outright. Nor could his suspicions about Athena.

"So you went back?" she asked.

"I had no choice. I wanted to run away, because I knew if I stayed they'd be watching me like a hawk. There'd be no way I could go to follow up any clues. I thought if I could get away I could use the money they'd paid her for having the baby to find them."

"That seems rather fitting."

"I thought so. But I knew if I ran away and then tried to access the money myself they'd find me, catch me and take me back or throw me in juvie. I was between the proverbial rock and a hard place."

"What did you do?"

"First, I tried to hire a private investigator."

She blinked. "You did?"

The idea of that determined fifteen-year-old boy walking into some private investigator's office floored her. At fifteen, getting through her courses at Athena had been her biggest problem. And if she'd had any trouble, she had her grandfather to turn to. Justin had had no one. She felt another tug of that growing admiration and began to wonder just how much trouble she was in.

"For a while, anyway," he said. "But I couldn't find a P.I. who'd take me seriously, either. Finally I went back to the nicest one and asked if he would at least make some phone calls for me. I told him all I needed was an adult to ask the questions, and I'd pay him as if he were out doing real P.I. work."

"And he did it?"

"Finally. That's how I found out Betsy Stone, his part-time nurse, also worked at Athena. And that all the hospital records showed that Kelly and her baby had died from complications during the birth." He let out a long, compressed breath. "The

P.I. said Dr. Reagan had a small, exclusive practice, and there was no breath of scandal attached to him. No one had anything negative to say." He paused. "I looked into Reagan myself, once I finished FBI training and was assigned to Arizona. Dr. Reagan had died a few years back from heart failure."

Alex stopped rubbing at her goose bump-covered skin. "Do you have a first name?"

"Yes. It was Henry. Dr. Henry Reagan. Why?"

"Nothing," Alex said, "just trying to keep everything straight."

But inside she was shaken. Very shaken. Although he likely didn't know it, Justin had just added a solid and very heavy block of credibility to what had seemed to be far-out and very unlikely speculation. But no longer could he be written off as simply an obsessed man driven by some childhood conspiracy theory. Nor could she deny that his sister's death and Rainy's were somehow connected.

Because Dr. Henry Reagan had been the name on the medical charts about Rainy's appendectomy.

"I've kept track of Athena Academy for years, hoping for a clue. I knew who Lorraine Carrington was. When I read about her death, I checked into it," he said.

"Rainy," Alex said. "Call her Rainy. She hated being called Lorraine."

"Oh."

He seemed disconcerted by that, as if knowing

her nickname made her more than just a name in a newspaper.

"And you?" he asked. "Are you Alex instead of Alexandra?"

She eyed him warningly. "For those I'm on a first-name basis with, yes."

"Okay, Ms. Forsythe," he said with a wry smile. "I saw you on television. That obnoxious bimbette of a reporter who cornered you all at the funeral."

Okay, points for that, Alex thought. Most men just saw the good-looking blonde part.

But she hadn't realized Shannon had actually put anything on the air. "She actually ran some of that tape? What could she possibly have used? We all creamed her, and surely she wouldn't put Tory's face on the air, when they're in such hot competition on rival networks."

"No," Justin said, "she got around that by just showing all of you on film and voicing over it herself. The only real sound bite she used was from you."

"Me?" That startled her.

"You don't seem the type who's hungry for notoriety, or to get her face on television."

Alex blinked. "What?"

"She played a clip where you asked—too disingenuously if you ask me—if you were really going to be on the news. Her voice-over implied that you were eager to be on TV, because most Athena graduates were upset that they weren't as famous as they had expected to be. Not in so many words, but the inference was definitely there."

Alex smothered a disgusted groan.

"I assume she edited you?" he asked.

Alex grimaced. "Oh, not much, only the part where I pointed out she's the only person ever to be kicked out of Athena, for incompetence, lying, stealing and trying to frame someone else for it."

His brows rose. "Really?" He looked thoughtful. "I didn't know she'd ever been a student at Athena at all. So, then, the subtext she was trying to plant must be that you're all jealous of her, because she's got face time on the little screen and you don't?"

Okay, more points for picking up on that so quickly, Alex thought. He was piling them up at a rapid rate.

"Probably," she muttered.

"Now isn't that just too interesting."

"What's interesting to me," Alex said, "is how she found out about the funeral at all. It wasn't announced or advertised."

As soon as she said the words, all the points she'd been mentally tallying for him suddenly weren't worth as much, and she asked him the question she now realized she should have thought of long ago.

"Which brings me to how you found out about it, in time to show up."

"Simple," he said. "I called the Pinal County sheriff, where the accident occurred. They knew."

"So you badged it out of them?"

"I hardly had to push. They had no reason not to cooperate," he said mildly.

"Of course not," she said dryly. Then another thought occurred to her, and her gaze narrowed as she looked at him. "What about the morgue?"

He blinked. "What?"

"The morgue. What were you doing there?" Her voice rose a fraction as the memory of that hand reaching for Rainy's body came back to her with the force of a blow. "What were you doing to Rainy?"

He frowned then. "I didn't do anything. I was never at the morgue, or even at the hospital. I thought it would call too much attention to my poking around on this. I'm already skating a fine line."

She stared at him for a long, silent moment, trying to decide if she believed him or not. She wanted to, and that scared her a little, given the effect he had on her.

"I won't say I didn't think about it," he admitted. "But I figured I'd just get a copy of the autopsy when it was filed, and that would be one less place I'd have to stick my nose into."

"Especially since you're not supposed to be sticking your nose in anywhere near this case." She didn't miss the faint grimace that tightened his mouth. "So how much trouble are you in?"

"Some," he said with a half shrug. "But not a lot. Not yet, anyway," he amended wryly. "Although you didn't help any, with that stunt yesterday."

"At the time, I thought you had it coming."

"And now?"

"Now, I haven't decided yet."

So, she thought, if he hadn't been the one in the morgue, then there was no way—or should be no way—he could know about the egg mining. And if he didn't know about the egg mining, then there was one more obvious question.

She asked it.

"What makes you think Rainy's death has anything to do with what happened to your sister?"

"I don't know if it does. I just know that anything suspicious having to do with Athena or anyone from Athena was something I wanted to check out. And then I heard the rumor that you and the others suspected it was murder—"

"Where did you hear that?" she asked sharply.

"Well, I didn't hear that in so many words, exactly," he said. "I heard from the locals that you were...having trouble accepting that it was an accident, I think was how they put it. And then when the reporter said you thought it was murder, I put it together."

"I'd like to know where the bimbette heard it," Alex muttered.

A trace of a smile flickered across his face before he continued. "Anyway, the more I dug, the stranger the whole thing got. And when I found out your friend had been going to a fertility specialist that occasionally recommended surrogates...."

He ended with a shrug, and Alex felt a little

burst of relief. He really didn't know about the egg mining. Assuming, of course, that he was telling the truth. But he'd been honest so far, at least as far as she knew. And while what he'd told her was hardly the basis for a rational investigation, she supposed it was enough for a man obsessed.

"So that's why you were poking around in Dr. Halburg's files?"

"That's why I went there. But like I said, the office was already a wreck when I got there today."

"So why were you at Athena?"

"Which time?" he asked.

She felt a drip of moisture from her glass run over her finger as another piece fell into place. "It was you, wasn't it? The other night at Athena?"

"You mean when you rode off into the mountains and were gone until daylight?" he asked sourly. "Yeah, that was me. All I wanted to do was talk to you."

"Why didn't you simply say so, then?"

"I knew that the fewer people who saw me on Athena grounds, the better. I didn't want to get caught there again, and be facing harassment charges or something. And you weren't alone that night in the barn."

Alex stifled a grin. "But I was."

"You were what?"

"Alone."

"Well, after the other woman left, yeah, and I started toward the barn, but by then you were coming out on that horse and I couldn't catch you on foot. So I—"

"There was no other woman."

"—watched and waited, until…. What did you say?"

"There was no other woman."

"I mean the woman who came out of the barn right after you went in and—" He stopped himself abruptly. He stared at her. "That was you? With the drawl? But she was smaller, shorter and—"

At her nod, his expression went from disbelief to sheepishness, followed by a slow shake of his head and the most rueful chuckle she'd ever heard.

"Damn," he said, "you're good."

"Okay, you get your points back," she said, and even when he looked at her quizzically she didn't explain. She didn't think she could, not without betraying more than she was ready to about how she was coming to feel about Agent Justin Cohen.

She drank the last of her tea with lemonade. She stirred up the ice that remained in the plastic cup. He'd already drained his frappuccino a few minutes ago. They sat in silence for a long time before he spoke again, and when he did his voice was quiet, almost gentle.

"From what little I've been able to find out since Kelly died and I've been focused on Athena, I've learned that it's a very special place."

"It's more than that," Alex said, responding to his tone. "It's a way of life, a goal, an achievement, a touchstone and…home."

She'd not often put it into words like that, and that she'd done it now, to a virtual stranger, surprised her. She was used to not talking about it to anyone on the outside at all, so this seemed doubly odd. But also necessary; perhaps if he understood, he would realize what he might be damaging with his relentless crusade.

As if he'd read her thoughts, he said, "I don't mean any harm to that. But I'm going to find out what really happened to my sister. I wish that it wasn't all tangled up with Athena, but I'm certain that it is."

Alex wished she could deny it, so vehemently and positively that he would be forced to believe it, forced to go away and leave them alone.

But she couldn't. She couldn't deny it at all, not with the knowledge she had about what had been done to Rainy. Athena, or someone there, could very well have been involved, just as Kayla had suspected.

And that tore at the very foundation of her life.

Just like his sister's death had destroyed the foundation of Justin's life?

The thought rose unbidden in her mind, tugging at the heart of the girl who'd once woven midnight fantasies about a darkly passionate young man.

And she told herself she'd better remember that there were two sides to all this.

And both sides had already lost a great deal.

Chapter 17

Alex felt numb. She went through the motions, got back into her car, slipped off her jacket and put her weapon back into the satchel holster, got in, started the engine, put it in gear, released the brake, exited the parking garage, negotiated the streets of Tucson, got on the right road to get to I-10 and back to Phoenix.

But she did it mechanically, feeling little, not even the heat. If she hadn't left it on when she'd turned off the car, she doubted she would be able to think clearly enough to turn on the air-conditioning.

She tried to think of a time, any time, when she'd felt this way. There was none. The closest she could come up with was when she was nine and they had feared G.C. was having a heart attack. The thought of losing him had been devastating, and the first real trauma of her sheltered life. She'd never really known her father, had seen little of him since he'd never been close to her or her brother, and his passing years ago had made barely a ripple in her life. The only thing she'd learned from it was that death was indeed final and forever, but since she'd never had to apply it to someone she really, truly loved, the lesson lay dormant, waiting.

But G.C. was something else, he was the cornerstone, the core around which all else had revolved in her child's world. She hadn't even had Athena then, not yet, so her grandfather was also the only center her life had had. As a child she had lived for the weekends and summers she and Ben spent with him, and only much later had she realized what he must have had to do, arranging his busy and complex business life, to be able to spend that much time with his grandchildren. And how he must have been trying to make up for the absence of his son, their father, in all of their lives.

The thought of losing her grandfather had terrified her beyond dealing with, and she had gone into complete, total denial, refusing to admit even to herself that it was happening at all. She had hidden from it, immersing herself in reading, music, television, even sneaking out of the house at night, wanting the intense concentration it took to get out unheard, anything that would help her pretend that grim reality wasn't out there, hovering.

But it had turned out to be something benign, she couldn't even remember now what, and her life had quickly settled back into its pleasant course as she pretended it had all been a bad dream or a mistake.

When the time came, after her brief rebellion, she went to Athena, and it gave her what had always been missing in any relationship outside of hers with her grandfather and sometimes her brother, a sense of tightly knit family, of people you could count on no matter what, of the kind of bonds built by choice rather than by familial ties.

Now that was being threatened. Athena was the place where she'd grown up, the place that had provided her the stability and structure she needed. It was the place her grandfather had helped fund and build, it was the kind of home she'd never had with her mother, the place closest to her heart outside of the farm.

It was everything she'd told Justin it was, and more.

And she was too old now to go into denial. Rainy was dead, and the answers to why were tied somehow to Athena. She would have to deal with it, not just hide out in her room and hope that it all went away. But she was honest enough with herself to admit that that was exactly what she wanted to do.

The only way that would be possible would be if she refused to believe anything Justin had told her. And while she still didn't trust him—he'd gone about this whole thing too crazily, and she was wary of anyone with an obsession, especially one that had lasted nearly twenty years. While she wasn't one hundred percent convinced everything he'd told her was the truth, she couldn't dismiss everything he'd said out of hand. If for no other reason than that single name of Doctor Henry Reagan.

Images unwound in her mind, images that could have been from a childhood dream come true. Sitting across a table from the Dark Angel, his attention focused completely on her as he poured out the story of his life. How many times had she—and countless others at Athena, no doubt—fantasized about just such an event? Dreamed of being the one, the only, that the Dark Angel trusted enough to tell the truth to? Of what it would feel like to be that chosen one?

But like so many childhood dreams that one day came true, this one had become real long after she'd stopped caring about it.

Oh, now there's some denial, that little voice in her head cried.

Her fingers tightened around the steering wheel.

Admit it, she told herself with the first spark of real feeling that had burned its way through the numbing chill, you don't trust him because you don't want to. Because then you have to face the effect he has on you. And the fact that you already feel more connected to him than to the man you're supposed to marry.

Once the burst of emotion had passed she was able to look at it more rationally, to realize that her undeniable attraction to him was only part of it. That she had more solid reasons not to take on faith everything Justin had told her, not the least of which was that people with obsessions rarely saw things regarding that obsession clearly. And since his had started so young, who knew what false assumptions he had made along the way that had brought him to the conclusions he'd reached?

She knew she was flailing, trying desperately to make sense of it all, to decide what to believe. But no matter what she did, no matter how she twisted and turned it, the same thoughts stubbornly kept returning. Not the least of which was, if it hadn't been Justin at the morgue that night, then who had it been? And what was Betsy Stone's part in it all?

By the time she got back to Athena, she had a theory. A horrific one. But it fit all the facts. And most of the conjecture.

She parked and went straight to her bungalow, still hardly feeling the heat. Once there she began to pace, running it all through her mind over and over again.

She needed to bounce this off someone. Someone who understood the importance, someone she didn't have to start from square one with.

Only one person came to mind. The same person she had once bounced all her big ideas off of. Kayla.

This was too big to let some old spat get in the way. She started toward the bungalow's phone, to avoid using the cell. That thought reminded her she'd turned her cell off after Kayla had called while she was with Justin, and she ran back to grab it out of her satchel and turn it back on. It immediately beeped a message at her.

Restraining her impatience she dialed her voice mail. And got what she'd half expected; an order, thinly disguised as a polite request, that she get back to D.C. ASAP. Like yesterday. They'd been swamped with new cases, and they needed her.

Not now, Alex groaned inwardly. There was nothing worse than stumbling just when you were hitting your stride over the jumps.

For an instant, she toyed with the idea of just calling in her resignation and staying here until this was finished. She hardly had to work for her living, after all. But she'd worked hard to get where she was, harder than many, simply because of who she was. She had to be better than everybody else before anyone would believe she or her grandfather hadn't bought her way in. And even then she ran into that prejudice so often it made her tired.

But she had also had her supporters, people who didn't care about the Forsythe name, people who believed in her and her abilities. She couldn't let them down.

The bureau had put a lot of time and money into training her, and had a reasonable expectation that it would pay off for them. She had also given her word, by swearing that oath, that she had entered into this office without any mental reservation.

That was not a promise she would break easily or lightly. A Forsythe was always as good as their word, G.C. often said. And she'd die before she'd let him down.

Later, she told herself. Worry about that later. Deal with the here and now.

She called Kayla's cell. She answered just before it went to voice mail.

"Lieutenant Ryan."

"It's Alex. I need...some of your time."

Kayla read the undertone in her voice. "Urgent?"

"Yes."

"Can you give me five, maybe ten minutes to wind something up here?"

"Good enough. Can you call me back on a secure phone?"

Bless her, she asked no questions. "I'll use the scrambler on my end. Where are you?"

"The bungalow."

"Got it."

It was a bit less than five minutes when the phone rang. Alex grabbed it in the middle of the first ring.

"What's up?" Kayla asked.

"I had a long talk with the Dark Angel today."

She hadn't meant to start there, but that's somehow what came pouring out first.

"What?" Kayla almost yelped.

"His name is Justin Cohen. He's the FBI agent who broke into the infirmary, the one I told you about. And I found him at Rainy's doctor's office today."

Kayla let out a low whistle. "The Dark Angel is FBI? How'd that happen?"

"I don't know. We never got to that, there was too much else."

"This isn't good news about the Dark Angel reappearing again after all these years, is it?"

"No. Very little of this is good news."

"I closed my door. Let me lock it and close the blinds, so no one's tempted to interrupt."

Alex heard her set the phone down, heard the tinny sound of metal blinds being flipped closed. Then Kayla was back.

"Okay. I'm sitting down and ready."

"First of all, I'm convinced now there's no connection to Rainy's legal work. There's just too much happening on the other front, and my gut's telling me that's where the answer is."

"All right," Kayla said, "we drop that and focus on the rest."

Just that easily, she took Alex's word. Alex took a breath, then plunged ahead. "Kayla, I need you to listen, hard, to a lot of stuff. And not say anything until I'm done."

"All right. Let's go."

And in more or less the order she'd learned it in, Alex told Kayla everything. It took a very long time. And Kayla was as good as her word, she said nothing but "Go ahead," whenever Alex had to pause to organize her thoughts or untangle something that had come out confusingly.

Alex tried to keep her opinion and suspicions and

conjecture out of it, merely telling her friend what had been said and what she'd learned elsewhere, differentiating between fact and supposition.

At long last, she was done.

"Damn." Kayla said nothing more for a very long time. But finally, in her organized fashion, she said, "All right, let's break it down. If we take what he told you as true, what do we have? Facts, Rainy is dead. Cohen's sister and her baby are dead."

Alex fell quickly into the old method they'd used long ago to work their way through complex problems. "Supposition, Rainy's eggs were mined. Fact, Kelly Cohen died being a surrogate."

"Supposition, Rainy's eggs were used."

"Fact, someone broke into the morgue and tried to steal Rainy's body."

"Supposition, it was to cover something up."

"Fact, someone broke into Rainy's fertility doctor's office. Supposition, or maybe probability, since it was the *C* files that were disturbed, is that they were looking for her file."

"And throw in the sizable coincidence that said doctor is out of town unexpectedly at the very moment we needed to talk to her," Kayla said.

"Yes, there's that, too. Then, fact, Rainy's supposed appendectomy was faked." Alex was pacing again, quickly, as if the speed helped her stay controlled as they batted through the incredible list.

"Also to cover something else up. Supposition, the egg mining."

"Fact, the same doctor that faked the medical records on Rainy was Kelly's physician."

"Supposition, they're connected somehow. Which means this is very long-term."

"Fact," Alex said, her voice tight, "Betsy Stone was involved in both cases."

She waited, and at last Kayla said it. "Supposition… Athena is involved."

"And the Dark Angel has been right all along."

Alex could think of nothing else to say, and it seemed Kayla was in the same boat, for the silence spun out over the line like an almost palpable thing. It was as if they were both sitting there watching the world they'd known and loved crumble around them.

"Alex?" Kayla's voice sounded small, as if she were weary beyond believing. Alex knew that feeling, all too well. "What if…there were more?"

Alex let out a long, compressed breath she hadn't really been aware of holding as Kayla voiced the thing she hadn't yet had the nerve to put words to.

"They mined a lot of eggs," she said. "More than they would ever need for just one fertilization."

"My God," Kayla whispered. "Stolen eggs, surrogate mothers…"

"Indeed."

After a moment Kayla asked, "Does he know all this? Cohen?"

"Not about the egg mining, or Rainy's connection. I wasn't about to tell him anything yet. His sister's baby died, so I didn't think he needed to know Rainy might have been the biological mother."

"All right," Kayla said briskly, "we need to plan what we do next."

"I," Alex said, "have to get myself back to D.C. or I won't have a job left. I got a rather fervent voice mail from my boss, and an e-mail to back it up."

"Then you'd better go," Kayla agreed. "I'll keep checking the files at Athena, and keep tabs on Rainy's doctor and go see her as soon as she returns."

"Good," Alex said.

"I'll question Betsy Stone, too," Kayla said. "I'll ask her about that Dr. Bradford Christine mentioned, see how she reacts. It'll probably be easier for me, you've had more personal contact with her than I, from when you—"

Kayla broke off suddenly. And with a flash of that old intuition that had always worked so well on two girls closer than sisters, Alex knew what had just hit her friend.

"Oh, Alex," Kayla said, her voice full of an emotion that warmed Alex. "I didn't remember until just now. You had an operation, too, when we were at Athena."

"Yes."

There was a pause before Kayla asked quietly, "Do you know?"

"No. Not yet."

"God, I'm sorry. How you must be feeling!"

"There's no use panicking until I know for sure," Alex said. Then, wryly, added, "At least, that's what I keep telling myself."

"I wish I'd remembered in time to give you a hug," Kayla said, for the first time since they'd reestablished communication sounding like her old, impulsive self.

"So do I," Alex said softly, acknowledging in tone if not so many words these first tentative steps back to their old friendship. But they had other decisions to make, and she went quickly back to the matter at hand. "What else?"

Kayla responded quickly. "The other possible surrogates. Let's call Darcy on that."

"I was going to call everyone, but why Darcy in particular?"

There was a moment's pause. "You didn't know? No, I guess you wouldn't have heard, she told me on the drive, before we all connected at the funeral. Darcy's running a private investigations business."

Alex blinked. "She is?"

"It's new, but off to a good start. She can check out the surrogate angle."

"Does that have something to do with her disguise at the funeral?"

Kayla's pause seemed slightly accusatory. "Darcy left her husband. He was abusive. But he's a powerful man, and she's hiding while she figures out how to legally be free of him."

Alex drew in a breath. "We'll help her. There must be something we can do."

"She hasn't accepted help so far." Kayla's tone had softened. "But I think starting this agency is part of her taking her life back. She'll let us know if she needs us."

"All right." Alex hesitated, then said quietly, "Kayla…if there were other surrogates, and things went differently…"

"I know. That's what we have to find out."

"I know. And we have to find out why."

They hung up, and Alex sank down into the chair beside the phone, her knees suddenly not strong enough to hold her. If and if and if…

Rainy could have a child.

Chapter 18

The flight from Phoenix back to Washington, D.C. had never seemed so long to Alex. And the last thing she wanted to do was go back to work, to hours in the lab wrestling with bits of trace evidence on cases from all over the country.

What she wanted was to stay on this case, this case that was lodged painfully near her heart. This was the case that counted, that mattered.

You sound like Justin, she thought. And didn't have the energy to deny it.

She had made the promised calls, but had only connected with Darcy. Josie was still on extended temporary duty and Tory was back on a news assignment and unreachable. She'd sent an e-mail to

Sam, and would check later for a reply. But right now, it was up to her, Kayla and Darcy.

By the time she landed in Washington, she was exhausted mentally and felt physically beaten. She even thought about taking a cab home so she wouldn't have to drive, but the hassle of coming back for her car later made her decide against it.

On the flight she had considered calling her grandfather when she arrived, but right now it was just too much to even think about telling him what was going on. He would be as devastated as she was over the grim possibilities of treachery and murder at Athena. And she just couldn't deal with that right now.

It wasn't until she had actually made it to bed that she remembered she couldn't have called him anyway, he was in Tokyo until tomorrow.

She told herself it was just as well, and laid her head on the pillow. She immediately went to sleep, but had she realized how haunted her dreams were going to be, she might have put it off a little longer.

Alex studied Emerson across the elegantly appointed formal dining table that her mother insisted on using even though there were only three of them.

Dinner with her mother was the last thing she wanted to be doing. But since she hadn't seen her in several weeks, and since she had caught up on her sleep last night, she had no real reason to say no. So she had dutifully agreed.

Her mother had requested that she invite Emerson, and that was a request Alex was glad to fulfill. She wanted the buffer. Her mother, predictably, adored Emerson, and Emerson made no secret of the fact that he thought Alex would do better—at what she wasn't quite sure—to emulate her mother more.

Right now the two of them, Emerson seated at her mother's right hand, her mother at the head of the table of course, were involved in an animated discussion. It concerned, as near as Alex could tell, the presumptuousness of some people. What particular group they were on now, she didn't know; she'd tuned out when they'd started in on those who wanted to join the DAR when their ancestor had been on the other side. Next would probably be upstart newcomers who wanted their grubby children in the pony club.

She supposed she could think of something she cared about less just now, but it would require more energy than she had to spare. And it was only worsened by the fact that she wanted desperately to be back in Arizona, digging deeper into Rainy's death.

"—are you, Alexandra? You seem miles away. Don't be rude, dear."

Really about two thousand miles, she thought. "I'm sorry," she said, belatedly spearing a bite of the asparagus with hollandaise that Margaret, the cook, was so very good at. "I was thinking about Rainy."

"I see," her mother said. "Well, that's understandable, I suppose. But really, it does no good to continue to dwell on the negative."

"Absolutely," Emerson said with a nod of agreement. "These things happen, but you have to move on."

If her mouth hadn't been full of asparagus, Alex was certain she would have gaped at them both. She wasn't really surprised at her mother, but Emerson's callousness had caught her off guard. It was probably just as well she had to swallow before she could speak; it gave her a moment to calm down. So when she spoke, looking at Emerson, her voice was carefully level.

"Is that what you tell the families of your patients that don't make it?"

Emerson had the grace to look abashed. "Of course not!"

"So you feel you don't have to be as kind to me as you are to them?"

"Alexandra, whatever are you saying?" her mother broke in, sounding more upset than she had when Alex had told her of Rainy's death in the first place. "Emerson said no such thing, he was merely pointing out that one can only grieve for so long. As I should know."

The reminder that she was a widow didn't come as often as it once had. Alex didn't recall her being particularly grief stricken when her husband, Alex's father, had died, but she had always tried to give her mother the benefit of the doubt by assuming she had been too young to really realize how the adults around her were reacting. Now, however, she was feeling less charitable, and more given to thinking she'd been right in the first place.

"No, Veronica," Emerson said, very gently. "Alexandra is right. I was unforgivably dismissive about the death of someone dear to her, something I would never do to a patient's family. I apologize, my dear."

And just like that, Alex remembered why she was engaged to this man, who could in a moment shed the air of quiet superiority and become one of the sweetest men she'd ever met.

"Accepted," she said, and he reached across the table to take her hand in his, those hands that had been one of the first things she'd noticed about him, even before his golden blond good looks. Hands you would expect on a world-class surgeon, long-fingered, lithe, supple.

They could be exquisite lover's hands, as well, and once she had looked forward to finding out if they were. Now she wasn't so sure. Now she was questioning the entire relationship, all because she was having a highly inappropriate reaction to a certain FBI agent.

She had expected his heart and mind to match those hands, and had only belatedly realized that he was so good because when he was in the O.R., the patient was no longer a person to him but a case history. She supposed that was the way it had to be, for him to continue to function on that kind of level.

Now she wondered if she'd just been rationalizing, going too far in her effort to see Emerson as the man she wanted him to be.

"Now that we've gotten over that," Veronica said, "are we ready for dessert?"

How very like her, Alex thought, to slide in that little dig at me, making my protest to Emerson sound like a childish whine.

"Your mother—" Emerson said as they finally left, or escaped, in Alex's view "—is the most charming woman. My mother already thinks a great deal of her. I think they're going to get along famously."

Alex winced inwardly at the idea of a mother-in-law as bad as her mother. Birds of a feather. But she managed to say evenly enough, "I imagine they will become very good friends." *Perhaps his mother will help keep my mother busy, give her less time to interfere in my life.*

With an effort she set aside her irritation with her mother, something she'd learned to do very well in her life. Something else Athena had given her—the self-control to choose her battles.

They drove back to her Alexandria home in Emerson's large Mercedes sedan. Alex relaxed into the rich leather front seat, letting the stress she always incurred visiting her mother seep away. Emerson drove competently, conservatively, and she knew they'd arrive safely.

When they arrived, he parked in her driveway near the steps and sidewalk to the front door. She no longer suggested he pull around back where he could park practically next to the back door. A Howland apparently never used the back door at any house he didn't own.

"Would you like to come in for a drink?" she asked.

"Thank you, no, dear. I have an early surgery in the morning."

"You could leave from here," she suggested. "It's closer to the hospital."

He frowned. "We've talked about this before, Alexandra. You know how I feel."

All the irritation she'd fought down seemed to bubble up anew. "Don't you have the least curiosity as to whether we'll suit sexually?" she asked bluntly, tired of dancing around the subject with him.

She thought she saw his jaw tighten, but his voice was perfectly calm when he said evenly, "I'm sure that won't be a problem."

She thought about trying to explain to him that she'd not been asking him for sex, but only asked him to stay because she was feeling very alone just now, that she felt as if life were careening out of control and she simply wanted someone there to talk to.

But with Emerson it smacked of begging, and she wouldn't stoop that low. She hid her tangled emotions behind a mask of mockery.

"A less confident woman rejected like that might question her own appeal."

"It has nothing to do with your appeal, Alexandra. You're a lovely woman, as I'm sure you know. But I'm hardly a boy who can't control his sexual appetite."

As if to prove his own words, he leaned forward and kissed her. It was a cool, gentle kiss, pleasant and affectionate but hardly full of passion. Alex kissed him back, rather fiercely, determined to see if she could wrest some sign out of him that this wasn't as easy as it seemed to be for him.

And then he straightened, smiled at her as if he'd noticed nothing out of the ordinary, said good-night and walked down the steps and to his car. He gave her a casual wave as he drove away. Only then did she admit she'd been trying to fire, in at least one of them, the same kind of passion that flowed in her each time she saw Justin Cohen.

Out of everything he'd said, one word echoed in her mind after he'd gone.

Control.

If she had to describe Emerson in one word, she supposed that would be it. Now she wondered if he might consider her, as his wife, one more thing to control. The night he'd suggested she would have to leave her job if she had children came back to her now, vividly and painfully.

She went to bed alone and lay awake long into the night. When she did sleep, she dreamed of times long past, of days spent at Athena, riding the trails in the mountains, watching the sunrise paint the world impossible shades of pink and orange and blue, feeling the cold desert quickly warming to the sun once more. Of Rainy, laughing, alive and proud of the group of women she'd single-handedly pulled together into the best team Athena had ever seen.

And she dreamed of children, all with Rainy's beauty and charm, her brilliance and her grace, helpless and lost out there in a heartless world that could conceive of such an evil plan, never knowing the joyous, wondrous person who had provided the basis for their lives.

And of Justin Cohen, wildly beautiful and passionately determined in his hunt for the truth.

She woke abruptly, and the remembered image was immediately replaced with a new one, the still charismatic, still passionate man the boy had become.

In those dark hours, she felt a kinship with him. She'd been girlishly awed by him then. She thought she understood him now. Because she, and the others, were in the same boat he'd been sailing alone for so long.

She tried to put him out of her mind, but he didn't want to go. He lingered, taunting her, reminding her of old imaginings long forgotten. She tried to think of something else. Wisps of her earlier dreams floated to the surface, visions of the children she had seen in that lost world. Rainy's children. Children Rainy had never known about. Children who had never known her.

Children, she thought as the mists of sleep gradually cleared, who might or might not exist.

Only then, as she came more awake, did a stunning thought hit her. All this time she'd been thinking of Rainy's babies, helpless babies, stolen from their mother before they were even conceived, implanted in a stranger, like Kelly Cohen, to then be given to some other stranger.

It hadn't occurred to her yet, the logical conclusion if the same thing had been done to her.

She could have children of her own out there.

She abruptly sat up. It was simply too much to get her mind around, at least right now. And, she told herself sternly, there was no point wasting energy on it when she didn't know yet if she'd been victimized in the same manner Rainy had been.

But her babies, out there, lost, alone…

And then, as her mind came fully out of the fog of those dreams, she got her second shock. She realized the true math. That if Rainy's eggs truly had been used for an in vitro process, and if it had been done at the time of harvesting, any child immediately implanted in a surrogate would be over twenty years old now. Rainy's child—or perhaps more than one—would be barely younger than Alex herself.

It made the search more crucial, somehow. It seemed even more important that they find out, so if there was a child, it didn't have to go another day without knowing about its true mother.

So she could only hope that, unlike Justin, it didn't take the Cassandras nearly twenty years to get to the bottom of their mystery.

* * *

For the first time since she'd been given her FBI badge and been sworn in as an agent, Alex hated her work. It took every bit of her considerable discipline to force herself to focus on the cases that she'd been handed two minutes after she'd walked in the door. A murder from Chicago, the latest in a string of killings from Atlanta, a kidnapping in Florida and a possible terrorist weapons cache in San Francisco. Her boss had made it clear they all had priority, and the load had kept her running all day long.

Each case deserves my best, she told herself sternly, trying to make herself concentrate. Her co-workers were no help, albeit with the best of intentions. Several of them, seeing she was back, stopped to express condolences, ask how she was doing and inevitably ask if there was anything they could do.

She felt like telling them they could take all this work off her hands so she could go back and finish what she'd started, but she knew they'd already worked hard for several days to cover her absence.

She set her jaw and began. She tackled each case methodically until she finally hit her rhythm and managed to push other thoughts out of her mind. Not that they didn't keep trying to pop up periodically, but she had managed to armor herself against them, knowing there was nothing she could do about them right now.

She matched the torn edge of a single piece of

duct tape that had been removed from a kidnap victim's mouth, to the end of a roll police had collected from a suspect's garage. The DNA from the victim was already in for comparison to that found on the tape, but this would give the investigators even more evidence. When she was done she filed the transparent film that preserved the tape with the rest of the documents in the submission package from a county sheriff in Wyoming.

She moved on to the next case, and the bit of glass removed from a hit-and-run victim's head wound. It was tiny, so this was going to take some time, she thought, but eventually she'd know if this fragment came from the broken windshield of the suspect's vehicle.

By the end of the day she had made good headway and had a feeling of satisfaction that she was holding up her end. Even her boss seemed pleased, although he couldn't seem to resist pointing out yet again how behind they were because she'd been gone so long. Of course, part of the reason he looked pleased was because she was still at her desk, clearly working, as he left for the day.

It was an hour or so after her boss had gone that her phone rang. She glanced at the clock, mentally crossed her fingers and reached for the receiver.

"Forsythe."

"Hello, my dear."

The sound of her grandfather's voice on the phone did a great deal to ease Alex's tension. She was glad she'd waited here at work, hoping he'd call as soon as his plane from Tokyo landed at 5:45 p.m.

"You're back?"

"Yes, although I'm still in New York at the moment. But your message sounded a bit…urgent. I thought I'd best call the first moment I had."

She'd called his voice mail that morning, indicating that she needed to talk to him, at length, alone and soon.

"It is urgent, but it's also not something I want to discuss over the phone."

"I see." His voice told her he indeed did see, at least, the importance of the situation. "My commuter flight leaves at 7:00 p.m. I should get in by 8:15. Shall I come straight to the house?"

She let out a sigh of relief. He would be there by nine. In less than three hours she could lighten this load by talking to the one man in the world whose opinion and intellect she respected more than any other.

"You won't be too tired?"

"I actually slept rather well on the flight," he assured her. "I'll be fine for some time yet. So, shall I come?"

"That would be perfect," she said, meaning it.

"Are you all right, Alexandra?"

It was the concern in his voice as much as his unusual use of her full name that told her he'd read the tone of her voice quite well.

"For the moment, yes," she said. "Now that I know you're on your way."

"I'll see you in a few hours, then." He paused, and then added softly, "Take care, Alex."

"I will, G.C. Drive carefully. I love you."

"And I you, my dear. More than I think you know."

She hung up, wondering why she'd felt compelled to tell him she loved him. It wasn't something they bandied about—Forsythes were not extravagantly demonstrative—but just now she'd been unable to resist the need to tell him what he meant to her. That he had returned the sentiment so feelingly told her he understood, and not for the first time she was very, very thankful she had him in her life.

Since she knew if she left now she'd only end up pacing the floor at home, she took the chance to do a bit more work. She set up everything she had to do tomorrow, so that when she came in she could go right to work. Finally at 7:30 p.m. she wrapped up, secured her desk and her lab station, logged the evidence, placed it into the security lockers and signed out.

At this hour the traffic on I-95 had eased somewhat, and she guessed barring any tie-ups, she would make it home in less than an hour.

When she arrived, she thought, she would turn on the exterior light over the back door for her grandfather. Unlike Emerson, Charles Forsythe had no problem with where he entered any house, as long as he was welcome. Then she'd put a kettle of water on the stove, because he'd probably prefer tea to coffee.

Or maybe, she thought with a sigh, she'd just go straight for the bourbon. That alone would warn him how serious what she had to tell him was.

She blinked several times to clear an odd bleariness that seemed to have affected her vision. She slowed and changed to the right-hand lane until it cleared.

She felt an odd wave of heat go through her. It was followed by a remarkable sensation of every last ounce of energy draining away from her. She wondered if the change of climate had had some odd effect. She should turn the air on after all, she thought, but somehow the knob was just too far away. Her arms were too heavy to lift. Too heavy to even move. Her legs wouldn't move, either, not even to hit the brakes, which she had a vague idea she should.

She'd never in her life been so tired. Nor had exhaustion ever hit her so suddenly. The last thing she remembered thinking was that it was odd that the car wouldn't stay between the lines. And then she couldn't even see the lines.

When the crash came, it seemed a far off, distant thing.

Chapter 19

"Let me by, that's my granddaughter!"

Alex heard G.C.'s voice long before she saw him. She also heard the sergeant who had been taking her information hurriedly tell the young officer who was trying to keep onlookers away to let Mr. Forsythe through. This was one of the few times in her life she was thoroughly grateful for the power the Forsythe name held in this part of the country.

"Hey, I know that guy." The paramedic, who was tidying up the small cut on her forehead that was the only apparent damage she'd sustained, had also glanced up at the sound of the voices. "Haven't I seen him on TV? And maybe in the paper?"

"Probably," Alex agreed.

"He's some real bigwig, isn't he? I think I even saw a photo of him with the president!"

"Right now," Alex said, "he's just my grandfather."

Charles had made his way to the paramedic van and was looking at her anxiously.

"Alex! They said you were all right," he said, eyeing the paramedic who stood there gaping with a pair of scissors and some gauze in his hands, with something like worry mixed with anger.

"I am," she assured him, with a dismissive gesture at her forehead. "It's just a little cut."

He turned to the young man, who seemed to be tongue-tied. Her grandfather often had this effect on people, even total strangers. Even if they hadn't seen him on television, in the paper or with the president.

"Is she all right?"

"I…er…yes, sir. She will be. It bled a lot, but she doesn't even need stitches." He lifted the gauze and scissors. "I was just going to put something over the cut."

She saw Charles look over toward her car. She didn't need to see it. As the young trooper who had first arrived at the scene had told her with a low whistle, she was lucky she'd managed to slow down before losing it altogether. As it was the car was a pretty sad sight. She had centered it on an overhanging sign pole, and had she been going faster, she could easily have ended up with the motor in her lap.

"What about concussion?"

Alex had already been through this with the medic, but let him answer. "We don't think so, there are no signs. She had her seat belt on, and that saved her from anything serious. We think the cut may just be from some flying glass."

"I'm lucky it only hit my hard head," Alex put in. "It could have ended up in my eye, and then I really would be hurting."

Her wry observation seemed to convince her grandfather she indeed was all right, because he immediately took charge and began to issue orders. Alex smothered a smile, not so much because he did it, she was used to that, but because people inevitably—and usually quickly—obeyed him without even thinking about who he was or whether or not he had any authority over them. Commanding presence again, she thought. Something some people never had to be taught, they were simply born with it. Charles Bennington Forsythe was one of those people.

Within a short time he had arranged for her car to be towed to the garage of his choice, even though it was all the way up in D.C., had the sergeant expedite the paperwork so he could take his granddaughter home and had the young trooper so in awe that he could barely speak at all. And for once, Alex let him. She was more shaken than she wanted to admit, and was glad he was there to take over.

It wasn't until she was ensconced safely in the front seat of her grandfather's big sedan that she told him what had happened.

"It must have been stress, from all that's been happening lately, or maybe just serious jet lag from crisscrossing the country," she said, "but it's never happened to me before. Not like that."

"Like what?" Charles asked, driving, she noticed, with extreme care, as if he weren't yet convinced she hadn't been damaged in some way.

"Like…just this enormous wave of fatigue. One minute I was fine, and the next, boom. It happened that fast, like…"

Her voice trailed off and she gave a little one-shouldered shrug. When she tried to describe it out loud, it sounded lame.

"Well, you're going to stay at the farm and rest, young lady, where I can keep an eye on you. And you'll be seeing a doctor first thing tomorrow to be certain there are no aftereffects. And I'll brook no argument from you."

"Yes, sir," Alex said meekly.

"You're obviously far too exhausted, for something like this to happen," he went on tenaciously.

"It wasn't—what did you say? For something like this to happen? Something like what?"

"To doze off at the wheel, of course."

She went very still. She hadn't thought of it in those words.

"That's what they said must have happened. You obviously weren't drunk, or under the influence of anything. Although I could have told them that without all their little breath tests."

Alex felt like a slow-witted fool. How could it

have taken her this long to realize? She fought
down a shudder that came from deep inside her.

She'd just had an accident nearly identical to
Rainy's.

And it was truly only luck, location and timing
that had kept it from having the same fatal result.

"My God," she whispered.

She'd been tired, but not that tired. Not tired
enough to just doze off while driving. In fact, anticipating the upcoming meeting with G.C., she'd
been awake and alert.

And she'd never fainted in her entire life, so that
was out.

Fainted. Blacked out.

One minute I was fine, then everything sort of
faded away.

Kayla's words, describing how she had blacked
out while checking the files at Athena, came back
to her now. She remembered the odd sensation of
distance she'd felt just before the crash.

Rainy.

Kayla.

And now her.

This was insane. It made no sense.

What the hell was going on?

Her mind asked the question, but her gut
screamed it already knew the answer.

Once is happenstance.

Twice is coincidence.

Third time is enemy action.

She tried to deny it, tried to tell herself it was

silly, that she was becoming melodramatic, that she'd lost all sense of logic and reality. But no matter what she told her reasoning mind, her gut was screaming again, utterly, totally convinced of one thing.

The Cassandras were under attack.

When they arrived at the house, it was her grandfather who went straight to the library for the bourbon. He poured himself a glass, began to reach for a second, presumably for her, then stopped.

"No," he said, putting the Waterford Westhampton decanter back on the polished silver tray. "I think tea will do for you," he said.

Alex started to tell him that she was fine, but she really didn't want alcohol fuzzing up her mind just now so she didn't protest. She also started to say she could fix her tea herself, but realized her grandfather needed something to do, so she let him.

The sight of him puttering around in the kitchen with a teakettle faintly amused her, as she was certain it would amuse others who knew only his sharp, brilliant, incisive public persona. When he opened the tea box and all he could find were tea bags, she saw one of the very rare glimpses of their aristocratic British ancestors in him when he wrinkled his nose.

"Sorry, G.C.," she said, stifling a smile, "I just don't have time to do it properly these days."

"Hmm. There's always time to do tea properly," he said, but fished out a bag nevertheless. "You go sit down in the library, and I'll be in directly with your tea."

She obeyed, with a quick side trip she was glad to be able to hide from him, into a bathroom for a look at the damage. She peered at her reflection. She looked a bit haggard, she noted honestly, but the cut really was small. She grimaced at the blood spattered on her silk shirt, but compared to the alternative outcome of being dead, it didn't matter much.

She hurried back to the library and curled up on the end of the sofa, leaving his preferred wing-chair recliner to her grandfather.

She loved this room with its hunter-green walls and rich-wood trim, precisely because it was the one place in this house where her grandfather's taste had reigned supreme. He had refused to let her grandmother "frill it up," as he put it, and banned any and all floral prints, functionless knickknacks, and curvy, delicate furniture. If it was in this room it served a purpose, whether a simple function like the carved jade pen cup, or the more intangible function of pleasing the eye or the hand by form or weight or being pleasant to the touch.

When he came in and handed her a teacup, she could tell by the aroma alone that he'd added her preferred honey and lemon.

"Thank you," she said, meaning it. The first sip warmed her throughout, and she let out a long breath, relaxing at last. But not for long, she knew, because it was time. Time to tell him the story that had ripped at the very foundation of her life. She knew it would do the same to him, but he had to know. Especially since that story may well have led to whatever had happened to her tonight.

As she had with Kayla, she asked him to just let her get it out. He nodded and she began. His expression gradually became more solemn, then severe, but as Kayla had, he only interrupted her a couple of times for clarification.

She mentioned Justin and was surprised when he recognized the name as the boy who had been caught at Athena so long ago. And her grandfather was surprised in turn when she told him Justin was now an FBI agent, had managed to get assigned to the Phoenix office, she suspected mainly to keep an eye on Athena.

And she pointed out that apparently Justin had been right all along.

"Vision, determination, passion and perseverance," he said. "Good qualities for a man. Or a woman."

He said nothing more, and she picked up where she'd left off. It seemed to take forever. When she was done, he asked another couple of questions, about things she only then realized she'd forgotten to include.

For a long time silence reigned in the elegant, masculine library. Alex stayed quiet, knowing by the way her grandfather had steepled his hands before him and the slightly unfocused look in his eyes that he was pondering, processing. That brilliant mind was at work, and she was content to simply sit and wait for the result.

She hadn't told him about her own fears, that her own reported appendectomy might have been a sham like Rainy's. She wasn't sure he even remembered that it had happened. It had been so long ago and he'd been out of the country at the time. And there didn't seem to be any point in burdening him with her fears when she wasn't yet certain there was any truth to them. She would see a doctor for more than just a post-accident checkup, have whatever tests were necessary, and then she would know. Then and only then would she add that into the confused mix. Or, if she was lucky, she wouldn't have to.

She sipped at her tea, a second cup her grandfather had prepared when she'd needed a break in her long discourse. It was well after midnight now, she noticed with surprise when she glanced at the heavy, cherry-framed clock above the mantle. She should be more tired than she was. She wondered with a little shiver if it had anything to do with whatever had happened to her just before the crash.

"All right," her grandfather said abruptly, and she immediately focused on him. "We have a string of mostly circumstantial evidence, some logical extrapolations, two confirmed deaths and three incidents or attacks on Athenan women that may or may not be connected. Out of that, we have a theory that, while it fits, may not be the only explanation for what has happened."

Leave it to him to sum it up in a mere fifty words, Alex thought. "That about covers it, yes," she said.

"So, what is wrong with the other explanations?"

"They require we accept a lot of coincidences."

"To play devil's advocate for a moment, isn't it a bit much to presume all these things are connected, part of some sort of conspiracy?"

"Yes," she said. It was nothing she hadn't thought of before. But in his life her grandfather had dealt with stranger things, with those rare genuine conspiracies of one sort or another that had spanned the globe, and she knew he was merely probing all the possibilities, not passing judgment.

"Before we accept this theory," he said, "there is one very large piece of information missing."

She knew there were gaps, but nothing that seemed so huge to her. "What's that?"

"The reason. The final goal. If it's true that babies were produced, from eggs harvested specifically from an Athenan woman…why? For what purpose?"

Alex went still. His questions smoked in her mind as if branded. Why indeed?

"We didn't take it that far," she said, her voice barely above a whisper. "We were so focused on the outrage of what had been done to Rainy, and wondering if she had a child out there, and if so how we would find it, that…we never took it to that logical conclusion."

"The range of possibilities is somewhat limited by the nature of what you've learned," he said.

"One is that someone is stealing eggs to produce babies for some kind of gain. Black market, perhaps?"

He nodded. "It's a possibility. Probably the most logical one. It's a big business, sad to say."

"Very sad. But…why Athena? Why Rainy?"

"I can only surmise the same answer applies to both. They chose Athena because that's where the best and brightest were, and they chose her because of her stellar attributes, even among those best and brightest."

It made sense. "I suppose if you're going to sell babies, you might as well sell good ones," Alex said, her voice sizzling with sickened contempt.

"It does make one wonder about the father, does it not?" her grandfather asked.

The father. She hadn't even thought of that. What man had been chosen as good enough to father the children of the finest example Athena had to offer? The whole thing smacked of something dark and twisted and evil, and Alex had to suppress a violent shudder.

"I wonder if he knows," she said when she was back under control once more.

"Another good question." He looked thoughtful again. "I wonder," he began, then stopped.

Alex's mouth twisted. "That's all I've been doing for days. You wonder what?"

"I wonder if Athena is the only place they did this?"

That was another one that hadn't occurred to

her. She thought about it for a moment. "I suppose they could have done it elsewhere. Any private boarding school could be a target, I guess."

"And Athena is hardly an easy target."

"No. Unless they had someone inside."

"Who could be Betsy Stone."

Or, as they'd discussed, Betsy could have been an unwitting pawn herself. Kayla would find out, one way or another.

When the silence stretched out for several minutes, he stood up. "It's time for you to rest."

She doubted she would sleep, not with all this tumbling around in her mind.

"I know it's difficult, my dear. Athena is as much a part of your life as mine, albeit in a different way. An attack on it is an attack on our very foundation. You must comfort yourself with the knowledge that this will not stand."

He said it with such confidence, such certainty, that Alex felt a slight relaxing of the huge knot of tension she'd been carrying around inside.

"You go to bed. I have some calls to make." Alex hesitated. "I'll report anything of relevance or interest to you in the morning," he promised, and at last she agreed.

She went upstairs pondering the marvel that was her grandfather. How many men his age could fly nearly seven thousand miles, fly some more, deal with a car accident, stay up later listening to and digesting an incredible story, process it and then make phone calls that would no doubt start the process of bringing the world—Athena, in this case—back into proper alignment?

Not many, she would guess. Not many half his age could do it.

Justin Cohen popped into her head. Now there was a driven man.

As she at last climbed into bed, she found herself thinking it was rather amazing that he had been so certain he was right at the tender age of fifteen. Certain enough to fight for his belief for nearly two decades.

Vision, determination, passion and perseverance.

Her grandfather's words echoed in her mind as she adjusted her pillow and let her head sink into it.

There it was again, she thought drowsily. That word. Passion.

Something Emerson seemed to lack.

And Justin had in abundance.

Chapter 20

Alex sat in Dr. Deanna Jorgenson's office, ordering herself not to get up and pace. So far it had worked, but she didn't know how long she could hold out. She knew the doctor had a lot of tests to go over—she'd spent an entire day undergoing them, after all, from X rays to ultrasounds to scans she wasn't even sure she knew the right name of, applied to every part of her. And the doctor had already pushed hard to get the results all back to her by today, so Alex couldn't complain about the wait, not really.

But that didn't stop her from feeling antsy now, wanting to get up and move.

You're waiting for news that could change your entire life, destroy your entire vision of your future, she told herself. No wonder you're on edge.

She had tried to concentrate on the mechanics of what she'd done today, had asked questions about each procedure, how it was done, what it would or could show. All to keep herself from thinking about the end result of it all. True, she wanted to know, but she also didn't want to know because of what it might do to her plans for the rest of her life, even those she hadn't made yet.

It wasn't a conscious decision to give up her quest to stay calm that had her leaping to her feet, rather she was already there and then surrendered to the need. She walked over to the window and looked down from the eleventh floor vantage point to the busy street below. This building was in a prime D.C. location.

Dr. Jorgenson had her own practice, but took referrals from the Bureau, and often did other work for them. She also managed to effectively walk the fine line between doctor-patient confidentiality when seeing an agent on a personal health matter, and reporting back when seeing them on an official Bureau referral.

Besides, Alex trusted her. And right now, that meant a lot. More than it ever had before. She'd never been so wary about who to trust before.

She heard the sound of the door behind her and spun around. Dr. Jorgenson, a petite woman with a bob of ash-blond hair touched with silver at the temples, walked into the room with a stack of folders and large envelopes of the kind that usually held X rays or other films. She plopped them down on the desk, sat down in her office chair and turned to look at Alex with a smile.

"Well, Alex, I could drag all these out and show them to you, and read you all the reports, but it would be rather pointless. With the exception of that cut on your forehead, and the safety belt bruise on your shoulder, you're in very good health."

Alex frowned. "I am?"

"Well, that's hardly the reaction I would hope for after giving a patient a clean bill of health."

"No, it's just…why did I nearly pass out the night of the accident?"

The doctor tapped a finger on the stack of documents and test results. "I could find no physical reason for that. At least, not a biological cause. Likely it was a combination of jet lag and stress, as you first suspected. Don't underestimate the effect they can have."

Under ordinary circumstances, Alex would have gladly accepted that explanation. But these circumstances were hardly ordinary.

"Dr. Jorgenson, I told you about my two friends," she began.

"I know. Believe me, I looked for anything suspicious that might explain what had happened to you. Even, as you requested, any sign of a mechanical device. It would have shown up on one of the scans. There was nothing, Alex."

Alex leaned back in the chair. She'd hoped for a simple explanation, but as with everything else that had happened since Rainy's call had brought the Cassandras back together, there was no such thing.

She supposed she should be glad that Dr. Jorgenson had taken her somewhat odd requests so matter-of-factly, not questioning but just doing. Perhaps she'd had stranger ones, over the years of dealing with the FBI.

"Now, about your other concern," Dr. Jorgenson said, and Alex sat up straight once more.

"Yes?" She waited, barely breathing.

"Your appendix truly has been removed."

There's the first hurdle, Alex thought.

"And, your reproductive organs seem perfectly healthy. No sign of abnormal scarring, and an appropriate number of random egg follicle scars for your age."

Alex drew in a long, deep breath and let it out, her body sagging into the chair in relief. Her future righted itself, and the thought of children of her own out there, somewhere, unknown to her and she unknown to them, receded.

"Thank you, Dr. Jorgenson. Thank you."

"My pleasure. It's always better to deliver good news." She tapped again on the stack of data. "But if you have any symptoms recur, anything even vaguely like you had that night, I want you to get in touch with me immediately. Don't brush it off. All right?"

"Yes, ma'am," Alex said dutifully.

When she finally left the office, she felt a new lightness that was almost heady in its intensity.

She was all right. Whatever had happened to Rainy, it hadn't happened to her. There would be children, if she wanted them.

Nothing could ease the pain of losing Rainy, and nothing could stop her from finding out the truth about what had happened to her, but for right now, Alex was nearly giddy with relief.

Instead of driving all the way back to the lab at Quantico as she'd originally planned, she called and let them know she'd just finished at the doctor's and was going home. She knew she was pushing the limits of her boss's patience, but one more day wouldn't break him. Besides, she'd pushed so hard since she'd come back from Arizona that she'd nearly cleared up her backlog already, so he had little reason to complain.

When she arrived at the house, she was surprised to find her grandfather there.

"I hope you don't mind, my dear."

"Of course not," she said, meaning it sincerely. "It's your house, after all. I was just surprised."

"I had business in the city, and it will continue into tomorrow, so I thought I'd come here and make sure that you were all right. You've just come from your appointment?"

"I'm glad you're here. You can help me celebrate."

"Celebrate? It was good news at the doctor, then?"

She nodded. "I'm fine. In excellent health in fact," she said. "Barring any recurrence of symptoms, I'm free to go about my business."

"Excellent," he said, as if he'd expected no

less. But the way his gaze lingered on her for a moment told her he'd been more concerned than he'd let on.

"Can I fix you some dinner tonight?"

"I thought we might play in the kitchen together," he suggested. "We used to do that rather well."

She grinned. "Yes, we did."

"I picked up some ground sirloin and ricotta."

"Ah. Do I smell lasagna?"

"Indeed you do," he agreed.

They fell into old routines easily, and as they worked a memory came back to her, an image of her ten-year-old self, working in the kitchen at the farm with her grandfather, solemnly telling him that unless she found a man just like him she was never going to get married.

Emerson Howland might be of the same social strata but he was nothing like Charles Forsythe.

Later, over a slice of celebratory cheesecake her grandfather had bought in anticipation of good medical news, Alex toyed with the glass that held her last sip of wine. And then, without even realizing it was on her mind or that she'd been about to say the words, she asked, "G.C.? What do you think of Emerson?"

He focused on her in an instant, and she felt as if his gaze was burning through her, analyzing why she had asked this particular question at this particular time.

"You're certain you want my answer to that?"

She hesitated, but that in itself made her realize she needed to hear what he had to say. "Yes."

"What do I think of him as a person, or as your fiancé?" he asked.

"Both," she said, still thinking perhaps she should have let this one lie. But she'd asked, so the least she could do was listen to the answer.

"I think he's a fine doctor, and likely a good man. He's bright, responsible and dedicated. He does good work that helps people."

"Is that the 'as a person' answer?" she asked, with some trepidation.

"In part, it's both. In fact, he's the kind of man I'm sure most men would be happy to see their granddaughters end up with."

She did not ask the obvious, did not question that "most," knowing he would get to it in his own time. It took him a few moments, but he did.

"But most men are not fortunate enough to have you as a granddaughter."

"You're saying…the thought of us together doesn't make you happy?"

"Whether it makes me happy isn't the issue. Your happiness is my main concern here. Which is why I'm giving you my opinion, now that you've asked. If you hadn't, I would never have spoken about it."

"Why?"

"You're an adult, Alex. Entitled to make your own decisions, without being preached to by your elders, no matter if they have your best interests at heart."

"You've never preached," Alex said. Her mother, on the other hand…

But if her grandfather had an opinion about his daughter-in-law, and Alex was sure he did, he kept it to himself, as he had for thirty years. The closest he'd ever come to admitting he didn't care for his only son's choice of a wife had come after that son's death, when Alex had begged to come live with him. He'd told her then that he understood why she asked, but that her place was with her mother. He'd promised her she would have as much time with him at the farm as could be managed. Then he had rearranged his entire life to accommodate her frequent visits.

"And the other part?" she finally asked.

"I feel that part of the reason Emerson is good at what he does, at least from my impression, is that he views the procedures as mechanical. Heart A powers body B and if valve C fails you do procedure D."

Alex's eyes widened. Despite having grown up with him, her grandfather's keen powers of perception still managed to astound her now and then.

"I'm very much afraid he would approach marriage in a similar fashion. And that, I fear, would not be enough for you, Alex."

Alex released a pent-up sigh. "You know me too well, G.C."

"You're not like your mother. Society and its niceties are not of primary importance to you." He didn't express an opinion, not really, but it was there in his voice. "You believe life is for living, and while the niceties are fine in their place, if they interfere with the way you wish to live, you quite properly jettison them. For some people, the social rules are their life."

"And you think Emerson is one of those?"

"I don't know him well enough to say, but I do know his parents and so suspect it, yes. He hasn't the fire you do, Alex. And I'm afraid it would result in you scorching him, or him trying to douse you."

Alex sighed.

"I'm sorry, my dear, but you did ask."

"No, don't apologize. You've only put into words what I've been feeling myself."

And that night, when she went to bed, she once again found herself thinking of that child who had sworn never to marry unless she found a man just like her grandfather. She'd meant it then, and in some ways it was an ideal she'd never quite surrendered. Her own thought of just the other day arose to haunt her, and she wondered if she'd been right to be half convinced they simply didn't make men like Charles Forsythe anymore.

But as she felt drowsiness at last begin to steal over her, the image that formed in her mind was of a dark-haired young man with the flare of passionate conviction in his voice, being led away in handcuffs. The image segued smoothly to the chiseled face of FBI Agent Justin Cohen.

Her final thought in the last moments before she slipped into a deep, calm sleep was, *Maybe they do still make them, after all.*

Chapter 21

Emerson's reaction when she met him for coffee after work and told him she wanted to break their engagement went a long way toward reassuring her that she'd made the right decision.

She hadn't expected him to make a scene—a Howland never would, of course—but he took it so calmly that it was almost an insult.

"I see. May I ask when you reached this decision?"

"It's been coming for some time. But to be fair to you, and to me, I needed to be sure."

"If I may hazard a guess, this began when your friend was killed?"

"What makes you say that?" she asked. It had

probably started before, but Rainy's death had brought it to a head.

"Because after that you became so distant and impatient."

The irony of this jabbed at her. "I thought you always said I was expecting too much closeness from you."

He had the grace to color slightly. "Well, yes, that's true. I'm merely remarking that the change in you was quite noticeable after you left for Arizona."

"If one of your dearest friends was murdered, wouldn't you be changed by it?"

"I suppose so."

He supposed so? Alex thought incredulously. And she began to feel a sense of startling relief.

"However," Emerson went on, "I would leave the investigating to the professionals, I wouldn't feel compelled to take it over myself."

She managed, barely, not to point out that she was a professional.

Positive—and now thankful—that she had made the right decision, Alex said, "I don't know what else to say, Emerson. I'm sorry, very sorry, but it's better to find out now than have to go through a divorce, isn't it?"

"Quite."

"It's just not the right thing for me."

"I think I know that. I begin to think it wouldn't be right for me, either."

She breathed a sigh of relief, but was curious enough to ask, "It wouldn't?"

"Quite frankly, Alexandra, I didn't know how much longer I could wait for you to settle down."

"Settle down?"

"Into a more seemly life for one of your position."

"Seemly?" she said, aware that she was beginning to sound like a parrot with only the ability to echo.

"Yes. More appropriate to your station in life."

She bit back the *My station?*

"More like your mother," Emerson said.

Ah, there it was at last.

If you're waiting for me to turn into my mother, you'll have a long, long wait, she thought. And realized for the first time that that was likely why he'd proposed in the first place, because he assumed she would turn into a younger replica of her mother.

"You mean give up my work completely, and concentrate on social events, being the famous physician's wife, entertaining your colleagues perhaps, nights at the ballet or opera, with some charity work on the side?"

"Exactly," he said with a smile of the kind you gave a child when it finally understood the lesson.

Alex sat there silently for a long moment, marveling how a man she'd known for so long, a man she had actually agreed to marry, could possibly know so little about her.

Of course, to be fair, she hadn't realized how far apart they were herself. Hadn't realized they were not just poles apart, but solar systems.

"Tell me something, Emerson," she said finally, "did the age difference between us ever bother you?"

"Not particularly, why?"

"So you don't feel twelve years between spouses is too much?"

"Not at all, once you're past a certain age."

"Good," she said, standing up and tossing money for her coffee on the table, seeing paying her own bill now as the seal on her new freedom. "Then you'll have no problem and can marry the woman you really want. She's only eleven years older than you are."

His regal brow furrowed. "Who on earth are you talking about?"

She grimaced. "My mother."

Alex walked out of the coffee shop and felt lighter than she had in months, as if she'd cut the last cord holding her to the world she'd never really wanted to be part of.

Only two things to juggle now, she thought as she got into her car. My job, and what happened to Rainy. And, she amended firmly, not necessarily in that order.

She'd hate to lose her job over this, but if she had to make a decision between it and pursuing the investigation into what had been done to Rainy and how it had led to her death—and the now very real possibility that there might be a child of Rainy's out there somewhere—then she knew which way she would choose. Luckily, she could afford to.

She frowned. Yes, she could afford to. But she wouldn't have the option if she were living solely on her rather paltry—relatively speaking—FBI

Forensic Scientist II salary. The other Cassandras weren't all so lucky. Oh, Tory was of course, but she had a career no one would ever expect her to give up and that could help in almost any case. And Josie was wedded to her career. But Darcy was obviously struggling, and Kayla didn't make a huge salary as a small-town police lieutenant. Sam she wasn't sure about. She had no idea how much the CIA paid.

If they paid by the IQ, Sam should be making more than the director, she thought with a wry smile.

It hit her then, how to solve several problems, including her own dilemma, one that she'd been wrestling with more frequently as her thirtieth birthday and control over her trust fund came closer and closer. Up until now, all she'd known was that she wasn't about to throw away those millions the way Ben was doing. She'd planned on turning a large portion of it over to her grandfather's financial planner; the man had managed to build G.C.'s fortune even through various economic downturns. She'd planned on buying a house of her own, eventually, although she was home so little she was in no rush. And of course she would donate back to Athena, she'd already planned that. Beyond those things, her wants were few.

She finally got the chance to pull out into the traffic on the street. She smiled, a genuine smile for the first time in so long it felt strange to be doing it. But she had made more than one decision this afternoon. And she liked them both.

She would take part of that multimillion dollar trust fund of hers and put it in a new fund for any of the Cassandras to draw on as needed. She knew she'd run into a brick wall if she ever tried to give any of her Athena sisters money, but this would be different. A sort of community kitty, mainly to handle any emergencies like this mess with Rainy, or heaven knew she could imagine them all having to go rescue Sam some day. But it would be a lot easier if none of them had to worry about money to do it. The traveling on Rainy's case alone was costing all the Cassandras money, and if there was a fund for that kind of thing, it would be one less thing for them all to worry about.

The more she thought about the idea, the more she liked it. She would bring it up with G.C. tonight at the house, she thought. He'd said he would still be there. He could advise her on the feasibility of it. And she thought he would like the whole idea, as well.

The next morning Alex arrived at work revved and ready, excited about her new plan, and about her release from what she could now clearly see would have been a disastrous marriage. G.C. had approved both, which meant a lot to her.

"You're finding your way, my dear, and I believe it's the right path," he had said. "I'm proud of you."

Nothing could have made her happier than hearing that from him.

On the other hand, her ears were still ringing from her mother's reaction.

"You *what?*" Veronica Forsythe had shouted.

"I called it off, Mother."

"The wedding? Impossible."

"Quite possible."

"You will change your mind, immediately."

"No, I will not. Ever."

"How dare you?" Her mother's shock had quickly turned to outrage.

"I dare," Alex said steadily, "because it's my life. Because it would have been a disastrous mistake, for both Emerson and me. Because half the reason I said yes in the first place was to do something right in your eyes."

And because there's somebody else who makes my senses hum in a way Emerson never could, she added silently, the image of Justin vivid in her mind.

"Don't be a fool, Alexandra. Emerson is the catch of the decade."

"I'm sure he will be, for someone." Unexpectedly amused at the idea of Emerson as a stepfather, she added, "I'm sure he'd appreciate you inviting him over to commiserate about your foolish daughter."

"Foolish and very imprudent," Veronica said. "As you always have been."

And proud of it, Alex muttered to herself. "Call him, Mother. He'd love to help you pick me apart."

And having done her part, she'd hung up, the old axiom about being able to chose your friends but being stuck with your family echoing in her head. And then she turned her attention back to other matters.

On her way in this morning she had made calls to Kayla and Darcy, to find out if anything had turned up in their investigations so far. Reaching only Kayla's voice mail and Darcy's answering machine, she left messages for both of them, indicating she had something to talk about, but making clear it had nothing, unfortunately, to do with the case.

She'd had little time to pursue that since she'd been home, and that was bothering her. She knew her boss—who had apparently already been here and had dumped another batch of cases on her desk—would give her that long-suffering, pained look if she asked for more time off, but she'd think of something, even if it meant flying cross-country every weekend. And in between she'd give her work here her focused attention, using the mental discipline she'd first learned at Athena.

She opened the first file, a child kidnap and murder case from Minnesota. She winced anew at the photographs. She'd vowed that, if she was ever able to look at the horrific evidence of what human beings could do to each other without feeling that instinctive recoil, she would quit.

She reviewed the evidence list. Thorough, she thought with approval. Sometimes those small agencies didn't have much experience with this kind of thing, but it appeared whoever had done the crime scene here knew what he was doing.

She'd already examined the hairs, of three different textures and colors. One they had identified as the victim's, which had been simple. The other two were unknowns but were likely from the suspects. At least, that's what the submitting agency thought. She hoped it would make their investigation easier when she told them the different colored hairs were actually from the same person, that their potential suspect had two-toned hair. Or had at the time of the murder, anyway.

The exam on the splinters of wood, found in the victim's hands, was going to take longer. She could only tell them so much, such as the species, without something to compare it to. According to the reports, the child's body had been found in a Dumpster, far from any trees, and they hadn't found the murder scene yet. But if she could tell them if it was maple or elm or ash or whatever, it might narrow down their search. Anything to help put the monster who had done this to a child away forever. She would start—

"This is more like it."

The deep voice from her doorway startled her.

"Much better than chasing each other all over, isn't it?"

Alex stared, unable to quite believe Justin Cohen was standing in her doorway.

He looked different in his deep-blue business suit, even though his position, lounging with one shoulder propped against the doorjamb, reminded her of the man she'd seen in Arizona. The suit made his eyes seem more blue, less green, but they were still striking. And in that instant, perhaps because she'd so recently seen Emerson, she saw the gaping difference between the two men. Emerson had little passion in him, Justin had enough for three men.

He stepped into the tiny office and closed the door behind him. Alex lifted a brow. It went up farther when he pulled over the single spare chair in the room, reversed it and straddled it. She wondered if he just wanted the back to lean on, or if he wanted it between them as armor of sorts. The way their previous encounters had gone, it could be either, she thought.

"You were just in the neighborhood?" she asked.

"I had a conference at headquarters, and thought I'd come by to see the new lab. They encourage us all to do that, you know," he pointed out reasonably.

She did know. And agents from all over were often in and out of the D.C. office for various reasons. She wondered if perhaps they had crossed paths sometime before and she just didn't realize it, because she wouldn't have known who he was. It had taken her long enough to realize it as it was.

As if he'd read her thoughts, he said, "I don't think we've run into each other here before."

"Maybe we have," she said, "and just don't remember."

One corner of his mouth quirked upward. "Not likely."

"Oh?"

"Running into you is not something I would have forgotten. Ever. Even if I hadn't spotted you that night at Athena seventeen years ago."

In that many words he had knocked the breath out of her in a way Emerson had never even come close to. The roughness in his voice sent a shiver racing along her nerves, startling her.

"I see," she said, suddenly realizing why Emerson had so often taken refuge in the phrase.

"I don't think you do," he said, his voice going husky as he added, "yet."

For a moment she simply stared at him, at a loss for words for one of the few times in her life.

"I'm here with a proposition for you," he said.

"So it seems," she muttered.

He grinned. It was devastating. Who would have thought the wild, grim Dark Angel would have such a killer grin?

"Well, that, too, eventually, but that's not what I'm talking about now."

She managed not to blush, but it was an effort. "Then what exactly do you mean, Mr. Cohen?"

"Justin, please. I mean, we've known each other nearly twenty years."

"We didn't even speak."

"Did we need to?"

Involuntarily Alex sucked in a breath and tried to conceal the movement. Somewhere along the way, the Dark Angel learned to be very, very smooth.

"Would you mind terribly getting to your point, if you have one?"

He lifted one dark brow at her, as if he somehow knew she only brought out the blueblood accent she'd grown up with on occasions when she was feeling personally threatened. Physically, she knew she could handle just about anything. Mentally, she dealt with most challenges with ease.

Emotionally, she had nowhere near that much faith in herself.

But when he answered, to her relief, he dropped the flirtatious bantering.

"I want to work with you."

"You do," she said, gesturing at the FBI ID hanging around his neck, knowing full well that wasn't what he'd meant.

"Okay, maybe I had that coming. But I mean it. We all want the same thing, don't we?"

"We?"

"You and your friends from Athena Academy. We all want the truth. Don't we?"

If the implication they might not want to find the truth was supposed to get a rise out of her, she was determined it would not.

"I'm still waiting for that point."

He stared at her, and slowly a smile curved his mouth. She didn't know if it was amused or amazed, but she couldn't doubt it was genuine.

"They grow them tough at Athena," he said softly.

"Keep it in mind."

The smile faded. His expression was solemn when he spoke again. "I want us to work together."

"On?"

"You know what I mean, but if you insist I'll spell it out. What happened to my sister and what happened to your friend are related. I'd stake my life on it."

"At a guess, you've already staked your career."

"As," he said, "have you."

She couldn't deny that. "What do you mean by work together?"

"Coordinate. Share information. Not sneak around each other, tripping over each other, with any one of us maybe having the one bit of information or evidence that could break it wide-open if it was combined with the rest, but not realizing it."

She couldn't argue with that. And he had a point. A good one.

"Not to mention," he said, his tone wry, "you and I being able to maybe space out asking for time off so neither one of us ends up on the carpet."

"There is that," she said, for the first time unable to resist a smile.

As if sensing he was wearing her down, he reached into an inner pocket in his suit coat. He pulled something out and leaned forward to put it down on her desk. She looked down at it.

It was a photograph. Slightly dog-eared, as if it had been taken out and looked at often. It was of a laughing, beautiful young woman with Justin's eyes. And in front of her, with her arms around him protectively, was a boy who was unmistakably Justin himself. But this Justin was also laughing, his face free of the tension and grimness it carried now. She'd seen a flash of this boy when he'd grinned just now, but only a flash. And she felt a sudden wish to have known this boy then.

Or to restore that joy to the man he was now.

"I will find out what happened to her. And I will not stop until I do." She looked up, met his steady gaze. And had no doubt that he would do exactly as he said. "And I believe none of you will stop until you find out what really happened to your friend."

"No, we won't." He had the measure of the Cassandras, all right.

"Then let's work together. We can do more, cover more ground, save time that might be wasted duplicating effort, and avoid antagonizing people who might get tired of being questioned twice."

"And avoid alerting those who might let something slip once, but would be suspicious about twice."

"Precisely."

Alex leaned back in her chair with her elbows on the worn arms, and steepled her fingers in front of her. He didn't hammer at her. He'd presented his case, now he waited for her decision. She appreciated that. Too many men would march in and start giving orders. Nothing was more guaranteed to get a Cassandra's back up than that.

"I can't speak for the others," she said.

"But you can speak to them."

"Yes."

"And your opinion will carry a lot of weight."

"Yes," she said, not bothering to deny the truth. "I'll talk to them."

"That's all I want."

"I can't guarantee how they'll feel about it."

"I understand. But what about you, Alex? How do you feel?"

She didn't comment on his use of the nickname that had been an issue between them before. They were beyond that at this point, she thought.

"I think we can probably work together," she said. "And that it would be beneficial to learning the truth about both Rainy and your sister." If I can keep my head where it's supposed to be, she added to herself.

He let out a relieved breath as he nodded, as if the entire issue was decided. As perhaps it was; he'd been right when he'd said her word would carry a lot of weight with the others. She knew if one of the others came to the group and said "We need to work with this guy," she and the rest of the Cassandras would trust her judgment.

Even, Alex realized, Kayla, whose judgment about men had once been highly suspect. And she realized thankfully that she was thinking she could really let go of that past now. Everyone made mistakes—she'd almost married Emerson Howland, for heaven's sake—and Kayla had obviously learned from hers. And as she'd said, if it wasn't for that big mistake, she wouldn't have Jazz, the best thing in her life.

Alex stood up. "I'll discuss it with those I can reach—we're all kind of scattered right now—and let you know what they decide."

Justin nodded. He turned to go. Took two steps toward the door. Alex had come out from behind her desk, intending to go out the door behind him, when he turned again. She nearly ran into him.

He didn't move out of her way. He just stood there, looking down at her. Alex was tall enough that she noticed when that happened. When he spoke, his voice had that rough edge that had sent a shiver up her spine.

"Remember when I said that was all I wanted?"

Almost numbly, she nodded.

"I lied," he said, and lowered his head.

She could have dodged it, could have stopped him, but she was so startled she didn't move. And the moment she realized what he was going to do a raging curiosity filled her. It was only in part fueled by the childhood imaginings of what it would be like to be kissed by the Dark Angel. The rest was purely and simply the man here before her now, darkly handsome and fiery with deeply felt passion. That he would have that same strength of passion in other areas was something she hadn't consciously thought about—perhaps hadn't dared—but she knew it had to have been there in her mind somewhere, near the surface, because when his mouth came down on hers, her first thought was one of recognition.

There it is.

It was also the last coherent thought she could muster. It was as if every nerve in her body awoke at once, some that had apparently been sleeping her whole life. They awoke and began to carry the heat he was generating with his mouth. She couldn't believe it was happening like this, it was just a simple kiss, he wasn't even pressing for more, wasn't pushing the kiss to a more intimate level. He was simply kissing her as if trying out the taste, lingering as if he liked what he'd found so far but was in no hurry to devour.

When he finally pulled back, Alex simply stared at him. He was breathing as though he'd run the FBI 10 point, six minute mile. She was pulling for air a bit herself. She thought he might do it again, thought in a rather scattered way that this was not the best place for this, but couldn't think for the life of her how to stop him. If she even wanted to.

"I've learned a lot of patience in the past twenty-one years," he whispered. "And right now that's a damned good thing."

This time he did go. Alex stared at the back of the office door he'd closed behind him, as if he'd known it was going to take her a moment to recover. She hoped it was because he'd been feeling like this himself, shaken and stirred, and a little stunned.

She couldn't remember where she'd been headed. So instead she went back to her desk and sat down. For a long time she stayed there, her mind racing in so many directions she gave up trying to clamp down on it. The only thing she could remember clearly was her own thought on the day he'd followed her at Athena, before she'd known who he was. She'd thought then that whoever he was, he was a threat to someone or something she held dear. She never would have guessed it was she herself he would threaten, and that he'd do it with a single kiss that would about knock her socks off.

When she finally reached for the phone to call the other Cassandras, to tell them that they were no longer alone in their hunt, she was smiling.

And somehow she thought Rainy would have approved.

Books by Justine Davis

Silhouette Bombshell

Proof #2

Silhouette Intimate Moments

*Trinity Street West
†Redstone, Incorporated

ATHENA FORCE

Chosen for their talents.
Trained to be the best.

Expected to change the world.

The women of Athena Academy
share an unforgettable experience
and an unbreakable bond—until
one of their own is murdered.

The adventure begins with these six books:

PROOF by Justine Davis, July 2004

ALIAS by Amy J. Fetzer, August 2004

EXPOSED by Katherine Garbera,
September 2004

DOUBLE-CROSS by Meredith Fletcher,
October 2004

PURSUED by Catherine Mann, November 2004

JUSTICE by Debra Webb, December 2004

**And look for six more Athena Force stories
January to June 2005.**

Available at your favorite retail outlet.

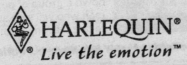

Silhouette
-BOMBSHELL-

introduces a richly imaginative miniseries
from veteran author

EVELYN VAUGHN

**The Grail Keepers—Going for the grail
with the goddess on their side**

Don't miss modern-day goddess Maggie Sanger's
first appearance in

A.K.A. GODDESS

August 2004

Is Maggie Sanger's special
calling a gift or a curse?
The ability to find mysterious
and ancient grails and protect
them from destruction is in
her blood. But when her
research is stolen and
suspicion falls on her
ex-lover, Maggie must
uncover the truth about
her birthright and face
down a group of powerful
men who will stop at nothing
to see that she fails....

Available at your favorite retail outlet.

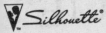

INTIMATE MOMENTS™

From *New York Times* Bestselling Author

HEATHER GRAHAM
IN THE DARK

(Silhouette Intimate Moments #1309)

After she'd stumbled onto the body of a dead woman, Alexandra McCord's working paradise had turned into a nightmare. With a hurricane raging, Alex was stranded with her ex-husband, David Denham—the man she'd never forgotten. And even though his sudden return cast doubt on his motives, Alex had no choice but to trust in the safety of his embrace. Because a murderer was walking among them and no matter what, she knew her heart—or her life—would be forfeit.

Available at your favorite retail outlet.

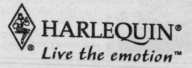

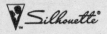

Silhouette®
BOMBSHELL

COMING NEXT MONTH

#5 KISS OF THE BLUE DRAGON—Julie Beard
Angel Baker wasn't your typical twenty-second-century girl—she was trying to rid the world of crime and have a life. Then her mother was kidnapped and Angel was forced to rely on powers she didn't know she possessed, and was drawn to the one sexy detective she shouldn't be....

#6 ALIAS—Amy J. Fetzer
An Athena Force Adventure
Darcy Steele was once the kind of woman friends counted on, until her bad marriage forced her to live in hiding. But when a killer threatened the lives of her former schoolmates, she had to help, even if it meant risking her life—and her heart—again.

#7 A.K.A. GODDESS—Evelyn Vaughan
The Grail Keepers
Modern-day grail keeper Maggie Sanger was on a quest, charged with recovering the lost chalices of female power. But when her research was stolen and suspicion fell on her ex-lover, Maggie was challenged to uncover the truth about the legacy she'd been born into—and the man she once loved.

#8 URBAN LEGEND—Erica Orloff
Tessa Van Doren owned the hottest nightclub in all of Manhattan, but rumors swirled around that she was a vampire. Little did anyone know this creature of the night had a cause to down the criminals who had killed her lover. Not even rugged cop Tony Flynn, who stalked her night after night....